A SMUGGLERS' TOWN MYSTERY

# The Thirteenth Box

J.A. Ratcliffe

© 2011 Julie Ratcliffe
Published by High Sails Publications
PO Box 7575, Christchurch, BH23 9HJ
Tel: +44 (0)1202 471097
www.highsailspublications.co.uk

First published 2011 by High Sails Publications
ISBN: 978-0-9568572-0-0

British Library Cataloguing in Publication Data
A catalogue record for this book is available from the British
Library

Illustrations and cover artwork © Domini Deane
www.dominideane.com

Author photograph © Amanda Clay
www.clayphotography.co.uk

Set by www.beamreachuk.co.uk
Printed by www.beamreachuk.co.uk

# Contents

# Acknowledgements

Whilst writing this book I have received much support from my family and friends. My thanks go first to my husband and sons who must, at times, have thought they'd acquired three new family members in Danny, Will and Perinne. Thanks also go to the following: author Judy Hall for her unstinting support, author Gwynneth Ashby for her valued guidance and to the members of The Village Writers for listening and for their encouragement; to Michael Andrews, local historian, for his support and for ensuring my vision of Christchurch in the late 18th century stayed on track; to Julie and Tim Musk of Roving Press. Also, thanks go to my sister, Wendy Edmond, and my great niece, Natasha Allen, for their invaluable feedback.

I would also like to thank Domini Deane for creating the wonderful cover artwork and illustrations.

For Mum who taught me to read and to love to read.

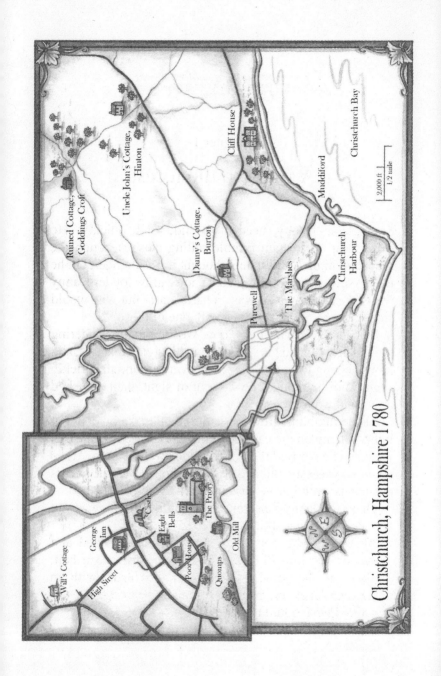

Christchurch, Hampshire 1780

Chapter 1

# A fright in the forest

Smugglers! Danny needed to hide and quickly. He could hear the distant rumble rolling closer through the moonless night. At first he'd thought it was thunder, but he hadn't seen any lightning. As the noise grew louder Danny realised exactly what it was - a barrel cart - but why would smugglers be out at this time with one of those?

He had to get off the track, now. Worried about wandering too far, he wrapped his scarf around his right hand and held it out, feeling for gorse. He felt his way around the prickly stems until he thought he was out of sight, then crouched down and waited.

As the rumbling grew louder he could make out a pin of light - a lamp on the cart, he thought. Then he saw the cart itself and he worried if he were hidden well enough. All he could do was stay still and quiet. He hoped the cart and its occupants would drive past and he'd be all right.

Then, to Danny's horror, a cry suddenly bellowed out above the Forest's stillness.

'Whooaa!' The hooves of four horses scratched and grated on the gravelly track as the cart drew to a halt, just beyond the gorse. It was larger than usual with an arched canvas cover, making it as tall as a carriage. Danny wondered what could be inside.

A man's voice boomed out. 'Hurry!'

Another replied, 'Aye, aye, I'll only be a minute!'

'I told ye not to go to the George. Couldn't ye stay off the ale for just one night?' the first man grumbled.

Luckily the cart and its flickering lamp had stopped just past Danny. He took a huge breath and held it, terrified that even his breathing would alert the men. He could feel his heart pounding in his chest, his throat dry with fear but he daren't swallow. He heard the sound from close by of one of the men taking a pee.

Suddenly the bag he was carrying slipped from his shoulder. Danny managed to catch it with his arm and hold it to his hip before it hit the ground. That was close!

'What was that?' called the man. One of the horses snorted and the chains on the harnesses jingled.

The man was close enough now for Danny to make out his tall shape. Despite the dim light, he feared the man might just spot him.

'It'll be rabbits. Come on, we must get ahead! We need to get to Winchester before daylight,' shouted the first man. 'Come on!'

Danny heard the man's boots crunching on the step up to the seat at the cart's front. A whip cracked. 'Go on!' came the shout, then, with a second snap, the horses sprang briskly away. The rumbling began again, this time getting quieter as the cart became more distant.

Fearing the riding officers would soon be on the smugglers' heels, Danny kept still. His heartbeat was returning to normal. He noticed his breath was making a stream of mist and thanked the stars he'd not been spotted. After a little while he stood up and stretched. His legs were hurting from crouching down and they were still shaking from the fright he'd had. There were no other sounds as he made his way back to the road and continued his trek home, relieved.

As he trundled on he thought back to the men. Something wasn't right. If they were smugglers why were they on the road now? It was dark, but could only be around seven o'clock. Didn't smugglers travel around late at night? That's what Jack, his brother, always said. Probably because they were going to Winchester, which was a long way off. His father had to go there sometimes and was away for days. But didn't most of the tea and brandy brought into the bay go to the locals? He thought he'd heard his father say so. Surely smuggled goods for Winchester would come through easterly parts? And be there before daylight too? Maybe they were meeting someone. But he'd better put those thoughts aside and hurry home - he should have been home hours ago. If only he hadn't stayed out so long, but that wasn't his fault.

Danny had been returning from Hinton where he'd gone to collect some cloth. His Aunt Mary had been out when he'd arrived, and he realised he should have had something to eat and drink and gone back home. But Uncle John had distracted him with tales of his heroics at sea. When he'd arrived, his uncle was sitting by the window. His face was wrinkled and he had a thin nose and small, grey eyes. His long, white hair which reached to the middle of his back was tied in a pony tail. He wore a leather waistcoat over a shirt with frilled cuffs fraying on their embroidered edge. As he began his tale, Danny drew a stool alongside him.

'We were taking folks out from Poole to make a new life in Newfoundland. The crew were mixed, new and old hands. Cap'n set sail in calm weather and we expected a plain crossing. Maybe there'd be storms, 'specially mid-Atlantic, but nothing like the one we came to face. One day, a week in, the skies darkened and a northerly blew in. We were used to high winds in the Atlantic, but this time it were different. The travellers feared for their very lives. Some crew had a time calming 'em, 'specially the womenfolk, screaming and clinging to their little ones. Cap'n said to tell 'em he'd drown 'em himself if they didn't quieten down. The swell rose and rose. We began to get hit by waves, near reached the sky they did, three times as high as the Priory church. The sky grew blacker by the second and that's despite bein' mid-day. Then it started - hail, this size, sent from Hell.' Uncle John made his familiar fist shape as though holding a ball and continued.

'The sails were wound in, but some were already ripped apart. But those waves - high as mountains they were and, atop, you could see whales, each as big as the ship itself.'

Danny sat wide-eyed. Uncle John had never mentioned the whales before and the waves had been only twice as high as the Priory the last time he'd told this story.

'But with the skill o' the Cap'n and hard graft from the crew we came through it. We made it to Newfoundland without the loss of a soul. Save those who died natural.'

People made fun of Uncle John, but his stories were gripping and neither of them noticed the time passing. When they did, it was almost dark.

'Get thee home now, Danny lad,' Uncle John had said, his spindle-like fingers quickly pressing a pack of cloth into Danny's hands. 'Can't let you stay, your mother'd fret and your father'd see me put in the stocks.'

'Hmm, might have me in them too,' Danny wanted to say. Danny pushed the package of cloth into his leather bag and slung it over his shoulder. He looked up at the sky - stars were beginning to appear but the moon would be a while yet. He tightened his scarf around his neck and tucked his hands into his pockets. A cold wind was blowing across the Forest from the east, but Danny was dressed for the March weather. His socks came up well above his knees and his breeches well below and he was glad for once that he wore Jack's hand-me-downs that were too big for him. His thin shirt was covered by a thick woollen coat, his scarf kept his neck warm and he wore a comfy woollen cap. He knew that even if he were to get lost, he'd be fine, that is, apart from the wrath of his father when he did eventually get back home.

Ordinarily he'd be kicking stones as he went along, but tonight he strained to see the way ahead. Now the stones unsteadied him and the road he knew well in daylight was full of ruts - rough and tricky in the dark. Nor was the New Forest a good place to be at this hour; the smugglers moved their contraband around at night and they would kidnap boys found alone, or so his brother Jack had told him.

Danny would normally have cut across the fields to his Christchurch home, but this was now impossible. The sky was speckled with twinkling stars, but on a clear night like this it seemed even harder to see. He needed to keep to the cart track. This would lead him onto the road that passed between Burley and Christchurch, close to where his home stood. He'd been to Burley several times, but he preferred going to Poole to see the big ships of Uncle John's tales. He also often dreamt about going to see the King's fleet at Portsmouth. Regardless of his uncle's exaggerations he loved hearing his adventures.

The leather bag slipped off his shoulder and he hitched it back on again as he carefully made his way along the track. A sudden crackling in the bracken startled him, but he knew it would be just deer or maybe a pony or two, which wandered the Forest freely. He knew well the animals and their noises - the whinnying of the New Forest ponies, the timid and lighter-footed deer and stags scratching their antlers, the smaller animals such as the rabbits and the hares, which all made distinctive sounds.

Danny took a keen interest in everything natural, but most of all he loved science and travel. He'd heard about

Captain Cook and his voyages around the world, across the vast oceans to unknown lands. He'd love to do that. Except that Captain Cook had died last year. His father James Clarke had plans for both him and his brother Jack, so no apprenticeship on any ships for him. He wanted them to rise in society and there were more opportunities if they could get a good education. So, despite the family's lack of money, the boys were sent to school. Danny's father worked at Cliff House and helped run the estate. He made frequent trips to the larger towns, he'd even been to London. Danny's father's ambitions for his sons made him strict: 'for your own good' he often told them.

After his brush with the smugglers, Danny moved cautiously down the road, which gradually broadened out. He could soon smell the wood smoke from chimneys and see it rising straight into the still sky from a scatter of homes. Relieved, he spotted the familiar shape of Staple Cross and then faint lights began to appear from the little group of cottages where Danny lived with his family. A candle glimmered in the window of his cottage. He opened the small gate and crept up the path. Then, taking a deep breath, he lifted the latch and entered, resigned to hearing his punishment for being late home.

## Chapter 2

# Shots on the marsh

At the same time that Danny was saying goodbye to his Uncle John, Will Gibbs was sailing into the Run at high tide to bring in his catch. He lifted his oars from the water and took a brief rest whilst his small boat was carried along by the fast flow of the channel. The Run carried the ebb and flow of the tide in and out of Christchurch Harbour at Muddiford. He didn't like going out into the bay so late, but the sea bass were plentiful at this time of the year and he could get a better price for bass than for salmon and other harbour fish. It was one way of helping to feed the family.

He took up the oars and with his back to the town and its imposing Priory church he began rowing again. He noticed yellow lights flickering to his left on the marshes and shrugged; smugglers, he thought to himself and carried on rowing, bearing east to find the fork for the River Avon. He pulled at the oars wearily. His father had died three years ago and, at thirteen years old, he was the man of the household. He worked through the day as a net mender. Occasionally he joined the crew fishing. If the weather allowed when he finished, he would take his father's old, small boat and set out to fish for his family. Will's life was hard and dull and he longed to be free of his chores.

He shivered; his damp felt hat wasn't worth wearing.

As he worked his way along, he tried to ignore his aching shoulders and his mind was on getting home. His stomach felt tight with hunger. He knew his mother would have something ready and rabbit pie would be his choice tonight, if he had one.

Crack! A gunshot blasted out across the silence, shattering his thoughts of supper. Crack! and then another: crack! Shouts of men followed, echoing around the harbour. What was happening? Navy cutters couldn't get into through the narrow run and it was easy for the smugglers to hide in the marsh's many creeks. Maybe it was a fight between riding officers and smugglers. Without warning a boat with long oars splashing wildly came into Will's view. A face turned toward him and Will ducked down, fearful of getting involved. Had he been seen? But the boat sped off. Will sat upright and sighed with relief but there was still shouting in the distance, he decided to get away.

Will knew the harbour well and it was a difficult place to navigate. There were sandbanks and silting, but the water was high at the moment and he should have no trouble tonight. The large harbour not only was a watery way to the town but also was used to bring in contraband. Will didn't want to be hauled into the Chief Riding Officer's cottage in Bridge Street to explain himself, so he needed to move on.

He rowed by the east gable of the Priory and under the old bridge and, at last, arrived at the bank close to the scattering of homes on the western side of the river where he lived. He tucked the oars aside, reached out to a nearby branch and tied up the boat. The fish he'd caught were in a sack, their salty smell seeping through strongly enough to make Will eager to pass them on. As he pulled himself onto the bank he heard the familiar gruff bark of his dog, Sam, running to greet him.

'Hello, boy!' The dog jumped happily around Will's legs and Will swiftly lifted the sack of fish out of the way.

'Not for you!' Will knew he couldn't afford to lose a single fish.

His mother, Meg Gibbs stood with hands on hips. She'd been at the doorway for several minutes and had a thick woollen shawl pulled around her shoulders against the chill. Her long, dark skirts were brushing the grass either side of the door which was closed, so that as little as possible of the precious warm air might escape. She sighed with relief at the sound of Sam's happy barks, knowing it was Will he was greeting. She hated it when he went out to sea, much preferring him to stay on the river or in the calm of the harbour.

She wished that he'd not had to grow up so quickly. But she was proud that he had work and that he could help to provide for the family and poor roof they had over their heads. She earned a little herself from making stockings, but this work was getting harder as her eyesight was failing. Will's older sister, Beth, also helped with her work at the George, but she turned many a man's head and Meg feared her hand would soon be asked for and she would be off and married.

As the boy and dog walked the few yards to the small cottage, Meg still couldn't make them out, but Will could see his mother waiting in its dim light.

'Hello, I'm back!'

Meg smiled as he finally came into view and she walked out to meet him. 'How've ye done? Beth's ready to take them into town.'

Will handed the sack of fish over to his mother and laughed as her arm fell with the weight.

'I think I'll 'ave to go with her, there's a good number,'

he said, taking back the sack.

'No, ye've done enough, ye need to be in the warm and dry. Go on in and get some broth and a rest. I'll go with her,' she scolded. Will sighed - broth, again.

He thought it best not to mention the shots, his mother worried enough. Will's mother was much shorter than Will who would probably reach six feet tall before long and he leaned over her to push open the door. As they turned to go into the cottage there was a loud shout. 'Meg! Meg Gibbs!'

A crooked old man was leaning on a bent stick. He wore a farmer's smock and thick woollen stockings, over these he had a gentleman's waistcoat and on his head he wore a curly grey wig which was coming unstitched. His small, skinny frame was topped with a tall but crumpled hat and he grinned, glassy-eyed, as he swayed from side to side.

Meg turned to the call, then immediately turned back, lifting her eyes towards the sky in contempt before continuing into the house. 'Come on, Will, let's get in. I'm not in the mood for old Isaac and his drunken ways.'

Will, laughing at the sight, entered the cottage and quickly closed the door behind them. Relieved he was finally home, he didn't want to bother about the antics of their strange neighbour.

Inside the cottage was small and smelled of wood smoke and tallow. Meg went to the window at the side of the door and lifted off the sill the candle she'd lit to guide Will the short walk from the riverbank. She then pulled across a dark blue curtain to keep out the night, and Isaac. A small fire burned in the grate and a pretty young girl, wearing a faded red dress, sat stroking Sam, who should have gone into the yard behind the house but had pushed through the door with them.

'A good catch tonight, Will?' The candle light illuminated Will's handsome face. His brown hair was swept back in a short pony tail and held with black ribbon. His dark brown eyes sparkled, but he had tired, dark circles underneath.

'Hello, Beth, yes, some o' good size. Landlord should give a fair price for 'em.'

Will handed the sack to his sister, but Meg moved over and promptly took it from her.

'Not before I've taken one fer us!'

Will glanced at Beth, smiled and followed his mother into the only other room on the ground floor, where there was a table and shabby cupboards. A pot over the fire was giving off light steam and Will went over and lifted the lid, breathing in the flavours. They might be poor but his mother knew about herbs and the broth would do, despite not being a tasty rabbit pie.

'Help yerself, Will, we've already had ours.' Meg bent to put the fish she'd selected into a cupboard close to the door. 'I'll go with Beth tonight. If old Isaac's rolling about I want to make sure she gets to work safely.'

'I'm sure Beth can 'andle Isaac! Think of the drunks she's to deal with,' Will said, chuckling as he ladled some of the broth into a bowl. 'Any bread for this?'

His mother offered him a chunk and placed a dish of butter on the table then went back into the other room to find her bonnet. Will heard a duet of goodbyes and the door closing. He finished his broth and went up the narrow wooden stepladder to a room in the roof where they all slept. He sat down on the low cot that was his bed, pulled off his boots and jacket and lay down. Beth and his mother slept at the other end and a thick drape hung from the rafters to separate them. It would be hours before they'd get home. He sighed at their poor lot.

Much of the work in the town was linked to fishing or sailing. His father had worked at Muddiford and then, prior to his death, close to the quayside by the old mill. Will had gone along with him to work as soon as he could. He'd wanted to go to school, but he could earn a few shillings helping with mending the fishing nets. His father had been a good man but was led easily by the likes of old Isaac and often money set aside was squandered. At least they'd kept out of the poor house. Well, for the time being at least. Meg's eyesight wasn't as good as it was and some of the stockings she made were not good enough to get the best money. Will dreaded the thought of the poor house. They'd be split up. He'd have to live with the men. In any case, he'd made a promise to his father that he'd care for his mother and sister.

'Why can't somethin' exciting happen fer once? Perhaps I should try smugglin',' he thought. Then, turning on his side, he pulled a blanket over his shoulders and fell sound asleep.

## Chapter 3

# A bully strikes

'Danny!' His mother's shout came as she ran quickly towards him and threw her arms around his slim frame. This surprise welcome was not what he'd expected.

'What happened? You should have been home well before dark.' Hannah Clarke's blue eyes glistened with tears of relief. She let go of Danny and took hold of the end of her apron and began twisting it. 'Have you seen Jack?'

'No, why, and where's father?' Danny asked.

'He's had to take some papers to Fordingbridge for Sir Charles, but he'll be back tomorrow. Jack hasn't come back from town either. I've been worried sick about you both - you could've been taken by the press gangs and sent to sea.'

Danny passed the bag to his mother. 'Sorry, mother. Anyway, we're too young for the gangs and I'm sure Jack'll be home soon, he's probably met up with someone and forgot the time, like I did. I just got talking to Uncle John, Aunt Mary was out.' He ran his hand through his wavy fair hair and smiled, his eyes the same blue as his mother's.

'Was she now?' Hannah Clarke was surprised her sister had not been there to meet Danny as she'd known he would be calling for the linen.

'Well, get inside and take off those clothes and get by the fire to warm. There's some bread, meat and cheese and

I made some muffins.' Hannah lifted the cloth from the bag and inspected it, 'Hmm, it'll do.'

Larger and much brighter than the Gibbs' home, Danny's house was set amongst a small crop of cottages on Tarrant's Estate. It was less than a mile north from the coast and less than two to the east from the small town of Christchurch. The ancient town sat between two rivers and was overlooked by the majestic Priory church. The Priory had stood at the harbour edge for 700 years and even escaped being destroyed by Henry VIII after pleas from the townsfolk. Nearby were the shell of an ancient house and also a medieval castle, which sat on a knoll close to the Priory. The castle lay in ruins, having been sacked by Cromwell's men over a hundred years ago. Danny had heard that stones from the ruins had been used to rebuild the George Inn, where coaches taking people to and from Poole and beyond called in for rest and refreshment. New houses were being built and the town was growing.

The cottage itself had both downstairs and upstairs rooms. It had a thatched roof and was fenced to allow chickens to run in the garden at the rear where vegetables were grown. At the front, Hannah grew a few flowers.

Inside, the parlour glowed with the light from oil lamps, giving the white painted walls a yellow, shadowy hue. There was a large, bright red rug on the floor with a polished table standing in the centre of it. Under the window looking out across the fields towards the sea, there was a bench with tapestry cushions patterned with leaves. This was Danny's favourite sitting place. In the corner of the room a shelf held a number of books including Danny's favourites, *Robinson Crusoe* and *Gulliver's Travels*. Danny had seen the pantomime of Robinson Crusoe at the theatre. There were also three books about the cities of Europe that the gentry now travelled to and that Danny loved to read.

A lively fire crackled in the grate and next to it, chewing

on a white clay pipe, Grandpa Hopkins sat in a wooden rocking chair, its runners creaking as he slowly moved to and fro. Sitting contentedly on a cushion next to him was Danny's sister Sarah, humming *Lavender's Blue, Dilly Dilly* and dancing a simple wooden doll on her lap.

Danny took off his coat, hat and scarf and laid them on a chair.

'Is that Danny?' Grandpa Hopkins said.

Danny walked over and touched his grandfather gently on the arm. Grandpa's sight had slowly got worse and he could barely see. He'd now lived with his family for a year.

'Hello, Grandpa.' Danny caught the sweet smell of the old man's tobacco. More often than not the pipe wasn't lit. Shreds of tobacco had fallen out and littered Grandpa's shirt.

'Hello Sarah, is it not bedtime?' Danny asked.

Sarah shook her head. She didn't like wearing her cap and her long, curly hair bobbed from side to side. 'Dilly doesn't want to go to bed, so we're playing.'

Grandpa smiled, 'Will you read to me tonight, Danny?'

Hannah had stopped pacing the room to fetch food for Danny. 'Let him eat first, father,' she said and set down a platter with the meat, cheese and bread on the table. Just as she was about to pass a cup of warm milk to Danny there was a sudden crash and the door was flung open. It was Jack. He had mud all over his clothes and cuts and bruises on his face. His breeches were torn and so was the sleeve of his jacket. He was hatless. And he was panting for breath.

The cup fell from Hannah's hand, hitting the rug and bouncing onto the stone floor shattering.

'What's happened?' she lifted her hands high, her mouth agape and eyes wide open.

Danny stood up as Grandpa shouted, 'Is it our Jack, is he harmed?'

'Yes, it's Jack, Grandpa, don't be alarmed,' Danny answered.

Sarah dropped Dilly and ran to her dishevelled brother and Hannah pulled out a chair and sat Jack upon it. Jack was two years older than Danny and much taller. Both boys had fair, wavy hair, but Jack's was now streaked with dirt. He was getting his breath back.

'I'm all right, I'm all right,' he repeated.

'Fetch some water and a cloth, please Danny,' Hannah pleaded.

Danny stroked Grandpa's arm again.

'It looks as though Jack's fallen, Grandpa, he's fine, don't worry,' said Danny and left the parlour for the kitchen, returning with a dish which he placed on the table. Sarah followed with a cloth.

'What happened?' Hannah said again. She took the cloth, and dipping it into the water began gently dabbing at the cuts on Jack's face.

'I fell.'

'It must have been a mighty tumble. Where were you?'

Jack pushed his lips together tightly. 'Ouch.'

'I want to know what happened, Jack. Look at you! What will your father have to say?'

Jack looked around, realising his father was absent.

'Where is father?' he asked.

Hannah breathed in, deciding whether to keep him in the dark for a while until she'd learned more about the evening's events.

'Fordingbridge,' Danny cut in, having left the room and returning this time with a broom to sweep up the broken china.

From the look his mother gave him, Danny knew that his last remark had been unhelpful.

Jack took a deep breath. 'I went to the Ship in Distress,' he confessed.

'What! Who with?'

'Thomas Burden.'

'You're fourteen, Jack, that place is full of people you do not want to mix with - ruffians.'

'I'm nearly fifteen! We only had small beer. Good people go there too!'

'Obviously not, seeing how you've come home! So how did you get like this in an alehouse?'

Hannah dabbed at the cuts.

'It wasn't in there. Ouch!'

'Then where were you and what happened? One more chance or your father will know you refused to tell me and deal with you on his return.'

'Don't tell father!'

'I'll tell father,' Sarah interrupted.

'What's happening? Hannah?' Grandpa Hopkins cut in anxiously.

Jack's eyes filled up with tears, something Danny rarely saw in his older brother.

'Our Jack's fallen, father,' Hannah tried not to let her concern show in her voice. 'And Sarah, you keep quiet.'

Jack sniffed. 'We, Tom and I, went onto the marsh.'

Hannah put the cloth back in the bowl and sat down, shaking her head with disbelief.

'It wasn't late, but we heard shots. Next a cart came past, the horses galloping, then four men came running towards us shouting. We hid and they didn't see us, but as we came back off the marsh a figure jumped out at us.'

'Did you see who?' Danny butted in.

'Shh,' his mother put her finger to her mouth.

Jack looked down; he was pulling at his fingers and then running them through his hair.

'It was Edmund Tarrant.'

It was Hannah's turn to take a deep breath and then she shook her head.

'Oh, Jack, don't tell me you've been fighting with Master Edmund again.'

'He started it! He said it was us shooting on the marsh. I told him it wasn't but he said it was us shooting at the birds. 'Where are our pistols then?' I said to him. He said we must have hidden them. I told him he was stupid and tried to get past. Two of his friends appeared and blocked our way. I pushed him and he punched me. Tom's in a worse state than me. They gave us both a kicking and ran off, laughing. I hate him!'

Hannah let out a long sigh. 'Both of you can go straight to your room now. My head's been spinning thinking what's become of you both and now this, trouble with the Tarrants. Your father'll be furious!'

'I haven't been in trouble!' Danny pitched in.

'You were late, out in the Forest alone.'

'Come on, Dan.' Jack took his brother's sleeve and they left the room.

The narrow wooden staircase led to a small landing. The two boys turned and went into the room they shared at the back of the house. The only light came from a small, four-paned window. The moon had now risen and its brightness illuminated two beds and a few pieces of wooden furniture.

'Now we're both in trouble with father,' said Danny, pulling off his boots. He tugged at his clothes, throwing them onto the floor, then slipping into a night shirt got under the bedcovers.

Jack made a pile of his muddy clothes and stood by the dresser. He wiped his arms and hands using water from a bowl on the dresser top, cleaning away the last traces of his bad luck. The floor boards creaked as Jack picked up his brother's discarded clothes and folded them onto a chair.

'Do you have to be so untidy, Dan?' Jack complained. Silence.

'You're not asleep, not that quickly. All you do is read those books and wander around the Forest. You'll never make a gentleman!'

'I don't want to be.' Danny turned and saw his brother's slight frame in the moonlight.

'I saw some smugglers tonight, I hid from them, they were going to Winchester,' he said.

'More romance,' Jack replied. 'I told you to watch out; you'll end up with the pirates on the high seas. Anyway, I heard lots of the stuff that gets smuggled in goes to Winchester.'

'Did you really hear shots, Jack?'

'Yes, three or four, in the distance.'

'Do you think it was Edmund Tarrant?'

'It wouldn't surprise me if it was. But I don't think so.'

Jack had now slipped into his own bed and pulled the woollen counterpane over his shoulders.

Danny sat up. 'Maybe it was the smugglers I saw who were being shot at on the marsh and they were escaping!'

Jack turned to try to get comfortable. His body had started to ache and he realised he hadn't eaten. 'Go to sleep, Danny.'

Images of smugglers floated in Danny's mind. What was going on? There was no school tomorrow, he'd go down to the marsh and investigate.

# Chapter 4

# A fishy meeting

Danny stirred. He'd taken a long time to get to sleep, excited at the thought of checking out the marsh and now he was wide awake and a different, softer daylight filtered into the room. Jack's gentle breathing was the only sound, he was still asleep. Good. Danny lifted his legs out of bed and went over to the dresser, intending to quickly wipe his face. He dipped the cloth in the basin and disturbed the mud at the bottom, making the water cloudy. He shrugged, left the cloth in the water and then pulled on his breeches, grabbed his shirt and boots then went downstairs and into the kitchen.

The clock pendulum swung rhythmically and then a chime rang the half-hour; it was six thirty.

'You're early,' his mother's voice met him.

'I thought I'd go down to Muddiford to see how many ships there are in the bay,' he said. He turned to his mother who was wearing the same look as the one that packed him and Jack off to bed last night.

'Oh, no you're not.'

For a moment, Danny wondered how his mother knew this wasn't where he planned to go.

'You'll do some chores for me. Empty the chamber pots on the dung heap, then wash your hands and face.'

Ugh! Danny hated having to do this smelly job. He

pulled on his shirt, slipped his feet into his boots and went back up the stairs. When he'd finished he returned the pots to their rooms and washed his hands. 'Eggs, please,' his mother then said, handing over a small basket made of reeds and lined with rags.

Danny sighed, took the basket and went into the garden. The chickens were roosting in a small wooden hut. Grandpa had built it to keep them safe from foxes. Danny lifted the latch and walked in. The chickens clucked quietly as he pushed his hand under the first and felt around. The feathers tickled the back of his hand and he soon found the first of the warm eggs. When he'd finished he counted eleven. He usually hid one or two to swap for things, but this morning he didn't keep any back as he needed to please his mother. His next task was to bring in logs from the pile for the fires. By the time Danny had left these in both the kitchen and the parlour, an egg had been boiled for him.

'Can I go after this?' he asked.

'You can go into Christchurch for me,' his mother glared.

'But that's Jack's job!'

'Jack isn't well, he was hurt last night and his ribs ache. Your father will be home tonight and I want some fish and a few other things. Can I trust you to fetch them for me and come home on time without getting into any scrapes?'

'Yes, mother.'

It was only about half an hour's walk into Christchurch. He could easily be there and back he thought. And then mother would be busy and he'd be free to go to the marsh.

Hannah gave Danny a list and the basket, this time with good cloth inside. She then pressed a purse into his hand which jingled with coins for the purchases.

Before long Danny was crossing over the first of the two old bridges that carried the road into town. The road often flooded when it had rained heavily or the tide was very high, but it was fine today. He saw Reeks' wagon pass by on its way to Lymington. He'd travelled on the wagon, which also took townsfolk to Ringwood and to Poole. It was a cold but bright day and spring flowers were beginning to appear. The green buds forming on the trees made dots of colour against the clear blue sky.

The Priory church towered above the town's buildings. Some buildings were of red brick with slate roofs, though many were still made of mud and daub with reed thatches that often caught fire. Christchurch was only small but had a myriad of different tradespeople who plied their wares along the High Street and the lanes around. Grocers, butchers and bakers and wine merchants had their shops. Smoke rose from the smithy where a blacksmith, a tall, bulky man, was forming a new horseshoe on his anvil. Shoemakers, bricklayers and carpenters crafted their skills as did the milliners and drapers. Danny enjoyed walking through the town and liked to watch people at work.

This time though he would cut past the old castle ruins just in case some of his school friends were in town for the market and would laugh at him carrying a basket. In any case he'd decided to go to the town's quayside first to buy the fish.

The smell of hops boiling in the town's breweries hung thickly in the air. Danny approached the Priory. He passed through the gate of a newly built wall enclosing the graveyard. He could see a few people milling around the Priory's arched porch. The vicar was there and Danny wondered what was happening. Skirting around the gravestones he found the answer. One had been recently carved with the name of a child, 'Lucy, daughter of John and Sarah Butler, 1778 – 1780'. Close by Danny noticed that soil had been disturbed, another recent burial, he thought. However, he needed to get on. He steered past the group of people and soon the water of the quayside came into view.

The sun caught the ripples of the Stour River and shone on the fishing boats, rocking like huge cradles in the water. The hop-laden air had now been blown away by the salty freshness of the harbour. There were rough-faced fishermen sitting beside their battered boats and people were looking into boxes which held the night's catch. Danny could smell the fish now and he wondered which of the boats to approach. He knew the sort of fish his mother bought and he didn't want to be too long. He looked longingly across the water towards the marsh. He was determined to go there today. He went to the first fisherman on the quay and chose a fish, wrapped it in the cloth and put it in the basket. He turned back and made his way towards the old mill at the end of the mill stream which, with the tide, drove its wheel. Danny was still peering over to the marsh, not looking where he was going.

'Hey! Watch out! 'A brown-haired boy with dark hazel eyes and sun-tanned skin, probably older than Danny, grabbed at the fishing net laid in swathes across his lap.

'Sorry!' Danny said.

'Can't ye look where ye're goin'?' Will Gibbs glared at him. 'Ye could've ruined me morning's work with yer clumsy big feet, cod's head!'

'I said sorry, didn't I? Ruffian!' Danny responded.

'What did ye call me? How dare thee!' Will threw the net off his knees and stood up, lifting his fists, in case the kid decided to go for him. A dog with a long white coat with tan patches, which had been sitting nearby, leapt up and began to bark.

'What's going on?' A shout came from behind Danny. It was the fisherman who'd sold him the fish. 'What's going on, Will?' he repeated.

'This clumsy goof walked right into the nets,' replied Will.

'I said I was sorry.' The last thing Danny needed was even more trouble.

'Get away wi' ye; shoo.' The fisherman swung his arm. Danny thought he might hit him and turned to run, but his left boot got caught in the end of the net. He tripped, trying to steady himself by putting out his right leg, but it skidded in the soft ground. The basket fell from his arm and the fish slewed out from the cloth, slithering across the grassy bank and dropped into the water with a splash. The dog chased after it, his tail wagging.

Danny despaired, then he tried to get up, but the boy held him down.

'Be still,' he shrilled. 'Leave it be Sam!' he shouted after the dog.

The fisherman stooped and was untangling the net from Danny's foot. Danny wriggled, keen to retrieve the fish from the water's edge.

'Keep thee still, I'll get yer fish.'

Danny watched, surprised, as the tall boy plucked the fish out of the water and picked up the cloth, carefully wrapped the fish again and gently put it into the basket.

His foot now free Danny tried to get up, but his ankle hurt and he winced. Will held out his hand. Danny, unsure at first, took it and was hoisted back to his feet.

'Thanks.'

'Sorry for shoutin',' Will said. 'I've a lot to do and I wanted to finish early today.'

'Thanks for getting the fish,' replied Danny, smiling up at Will, who was much taller than he was. 'You've probably saved my life!'

As Danny and Will shook hands another noise broke above the chatter of the quayside. From alongside the Priory a carriage appeared. It was the new type and could carry six people. It had leather strapping, the kind that made the ride more comfortable. It was drawn by four large, beautifully groomed horses, which had ribbons woven into their manes. Their heads were topped with green feather plumes, fluttering in the breeze. A coachman sat on a seat on the front pulling at the reins and by his side sat a footman, both dressed in green livery. The carriage was painted in a deep green and on the door, visible to Danny and Will, was the crest of the Tarrant family.

'Now there's a sight,' said Will.

'It's the Tarrant's coach,' said Danny.

Will looked at him, nodding.

'My father works on the estate,' Danny explained. 'I hope it's not Edmund.'

'Who's Edmund?'

'He's who you'd call a cod's head,' Danny grinned. 'He attacked my brother last night, which is why I'm buying fish this morning and not him. Edmund Tarrant accused him of shooting birds on the marsh and when Jack denied it, Edmund and his friends set upon him.'

'Oh?' said Will.

Danny wondered if he should be talking this way to a

stranger about the goings on of his family but then Will surprised him.

'What time were this?' he asked.

'Just after dark, I think. Why?'

'I 'eard shots on the marsh last night, I were on the 'arbour,' said Will. 'I were going to take a look after work. Were why I wanted to get done quickly.'

Before Danny could say anything more a boat with a small but billowing cream-coloured sail came into view. It was unusual. Not a coasting vessel but a ship's rowing boat. Two sailors wearing long trousers and jackets cut to the waist steered the boat to the short wooden pier. One jumped off with a rope and tied the boat to a post.

The footman from the coach was now on the pier. Trunks were lifted from the boat by the sailors and handed to the footman who had been joined by the coachman. Together they took four trunks and, one after another, tied them onto the coach. Then, from the coach a gentleman appeared. He had a round, plump face and his cheeks were red. He was wearing a rich, dark velvet coat with lace cuffs showing at the wrist and a lace ruff around his neck. His black breeches were drawn over white stockings and his leather shoes were topped with large silver buckles. He wore a tricorn hat with a plume of black feathers. It was Sir Charles Tarrant.

A crowd had now gathered, chattering in anticipation. Then, from the boat a woman appeared. By her side was a young girl, about Danny's age. They both wore dark, heavy cloaks and black hats. The sailors helped them onto the pier and Sir Charles moved over and took the lady's hand and raised it to his lips. He put his hand on the young girl's shoulder, gently shaking it, smiling. The group then walked to the carriage. The ladies were helped to climb inside, followed by Sir Charles. The doors were secured, the coachman and footman took their places and the carriage started off, the wheels grinding in the gravel as they turned. It then made its way back past the Priory.

'Well that were a sight,' scoffed Will.

Danny looked at him. 'I'm going to the marsh this afternoon. Shall we go together?'

Will, slightly amused, looked at the younger boy.

'Aye, why not?'

Chapter 5

# The mysterious machine

Perinne Menniere was shown to her room by a house maid in a striped green dress covered by a lace-edged apron. She sat on the bed as her trunk was set down at its foot by two porters; she yawned.

'Are you all right, Miss?' asked Lucy, who was not much older than Perinne.

'*Oui*, but I am bored,' she said.

'Well, Miss, you've had a long journey and it's some time before dinner. Why not rest. I'll come for you just before and help you get ready. Then we can unpack your trunk after you've eaten.'

'*Merci*, I mean, thank you,' Perinne replied.

The maid curtseyed and followed the porters out of the room, pulling the door closed behind her.

The twelve-year-old stood up, grabbed her hat and threw it across the room and, after pulling at the clasp, did the same with her cloak. She ripped at the laces of her boots and, after kicking them off, sprung herself backwards onto the bed. She looked up at the red silk folded canopy and the bed's four posts enclosing her and let out a long sigh; she wasn't going to let some maid tell her what to do. Jumping off the bed she unlocked and opened the trunk, pulling out an assortment of coats and dresses and throwing them onto the bed. At the bottom she found some slippers and pushed them on.

The room was square and bright with a mix of wooden panels and wallpaper adorning the walls. Rays of sun shone through a large window and Perinne walked over and looked outside, facing south, she thought. The day remained clear and sunny. In front there were formal gardens with box hedges. Beyond the hedges were lawns with swathes of sun-bright daffodils massed in patches across the grass, swaying lightly. There were trees, some coming into bud, both to the east and west but none ahead and Perinne could see why. Beyond the expanse of the grounds she could see the sea. It glistened and, on the horizon, were white rock stacks pointing out of the water.

She turned and looked at the room where there was an ornate dressing table upon which stood a patterned vase filled with daffodils. 'Oh, *non*', she thought. Her slippers were silent as she walked across the wooden floor and onto the rug where, next to a large wardrobe, a tall looking glass stood. She peered at herself then walked over to the door and left the room to explore the house. As she walked around she was not impressed with the grandness of Cliff House. Her grandpère had built houses like this and her own house also had carpets and clocks and paintings.

Downstairs, in the library, Sir Charles Tarrant was standing by a grand fireplace looking at the flames flitting around the logs in the grate. A silver-haired man was sitting in a leather chair near the fireside. Another tall, thin man with short fair hair was standing upright a few feet away, his hands behind his back.

'This isn't good. How did they know we'd be there?' Sir

Charles said.

'I don't know, sir,' answered James Clarke.

Sir Charles sucked in air, making a whistle, and exhaled, blowing out his ruddy cheeks.

'It pains me to think it could be someone in this house. So, are the boxes delivered now?'

'Yes, sir.'

'And is the place safe enough?'

'The house is in the Forest, too few folks to see any comings and goings there.'

'And you can trust these people?'

'With certainty, sir.'

'Excellent.' Sir Charles walked over to a large desk and opened one of the drawers. 'Thank you, James, I need to trust you to keep this quiet, from everyone,' he said, passing a cloth purse to his servant. 'But find out who these people are!'

'You can rely on me, Sir Charles.' Without looking inside, James Clarke put the purse into his jacket pocket.

'That should help your family, and, if we're successful, you'll be rewarded,' Sir Charles said, pointing to the pocket.

Sir Charles paused then took a breath. 'Madame Menniere and her daughter Perinne sailed into Christchurch Quay this morning. You've children, James, haven't you? What are their ages?' Sir Charles took a pipe from the desk and filled it with tobacco from a pouch, then walked over to the fire to light a spill.

'Our Jack's the eldest; he'll be fifteen after Easter. Daniel is nearly thirteen and Sarah is just six.'

'Hmm, pity the girl isn't older.' Sir Charles had lit his pipe and was sucking at the stem, then blowing the smoke towards the ceiling. 'That's all, you may go home, and thank you, you did the best that you could in the circumstances.' Sir Charles gestured towards the door and James Clarke knew to go immediately.

'Thank you, Sir.' He bowed and left the room.

'Well, Charles,' the man started, 'I feel we can trust Clarke. But how do we find out who they were and, what is more, who they were working for?'

Sir Charles shrugged. 'No idea. I've asked Clarke to get someone he can trust to ask questions around the alehouses.'

'Aye, the ale loosens men's tongues,' the man said.

'I'll also get him to handle any correspondence between us and the Royal Society in case it was someone in this house.'

Sir Charles walked over to a table that was holding glasses and a decanter. 'Drink?'

After a good look around the upper floors Perinne decided to not go down the main staircase and instead explored the rear of the house. She found a servant's staircase. The bare steps on the twisting stairs creaked as she made her way down them. Then she heard a door close. When she reached the bottom of the stairs she found a small, circular hallway with two doors. One led outside and had a narrow, plain window beside it, providing the only light to the dim passageway. The other door was propped open and Perinne imagined it led to the kitchens. The walls were plain, painted white with no hangings, but with simple sconces holding unlit candles. She could hear voices.

One she recognised as her maman's cousin, who'd met them off the launch. She'd seen him before at her home in France and had been told to call him Uncle Charles. At the foot of the staircase she noticed a break in the wall. She stepped quietly across as the voices seemed to come from here. It was another door and it was slightly ajar. As she approached she could smell tobacco smoke. She peered through the gap.

Inside she could see what looked like a library. There were books lining the walls apart from the one directly across from her, where there was a fireplace with a small fire burning in the grate. Uncle Charles was with a man she didn't know. Perrine watched as her uncle picked up a decanter of brandy. She moved as near to the door as she could and listened.

The stranger nodded. 'Now, tell me more about this machine,' he said.

Sir Charles handed him a glass of brandy and sat down in a chair facing the stranger. 'We've been told that with this machine people will be able to send messages through the air, from town to town, city to city. Imagine the use in battle; ship to ship at sea, general to general in the battlefield.'

'Incredible. And why haven't the French secured it?'

'Few know about it. My cousin tells me there may be unrest ahead, that's in addition to the wars between our countries. So when we heard it was being brought to England we thought it best to capture it and make sure it is sold to the right person. This country has many enemies, it would best be in our hands than theirs.'

'And your cousin, what part does he play in this?'

Sir Charles looked at him. 'He is a she, my cousin, Jane. She married Yves Menniere, a Frenchman, and lives in Rennes. His father's an architect and as an apprentice he helped to rebuild the city. There were dreadful fires there, though some 60 years ago now. Yves came to England to study and met my cousin. They have a daughter, Perinne.'

By the door, Perinne peered with interest, keeping as quiet as she could but she could feel her nose begin to itch. 'Those stupid flowers,' she thought and pinched her nose between her thumb and finger.

'Didn't the inventor file a patent?' the stranger asked.

'Tsssss ....'

Sir Charles looked around the room and at his visitor. 'The inventor, Costelot, was trying to sell the machine to the highest bidder but he was an arrogant man, started to talk about it too loudly around the taverns and coffee houses of Rennes. There were people who wanted the machine destroyed, it was witchcraft they said. A few weeks ago Costelot thought he was meeting a buyer, but he was attacked and killed. Then Jane and Yves overheard talk of the machine being brought to England to be sold here.' Sir Charles leaned forward. 'It was expected to come in through Southampton or Poole then Jane wrote to me about it. She told me they'd chosen Christchurch because of our harbour and it was being brought over a week earlier than planned. So I had men lay in wait on the marsh. When the gang appeared with their cart my men took them by surprise and tied them up. Then a boat arrived and they began to unload boxes, thinking the cart by the shore was their men. Shots were fired, a fight started. Seeing they were outnumbered they ran back to the boat and rowed away across the harbour, still holding half the cargo. We must find these other boxes!'

'And you think they're still in Christchurch?'

'Yes. Whoever it is they're working for will need to deliver the whole consignment. I have six boxes of parts, each box is numbered and there are thirteen boxes all together.'

The man swirled the brandy in his glass. 'How do you know this?

'Jane brought a paper, written in Costelot's hand. It says

that the thirteenth box is the final and the most important. We don't have it and it's the key to making the machine work.' Sir Charles seethed.

'But I've heard there are such machines invented already, using signals,' the man said.

'Yes, I believe so, but this machine is very different, as it transmits the voice. Whoever gets the machine, completes it and proves it works not only will have riches beyond his dreams, but hold great power in his hands!'

The stranger looked at Sir Charles. 'No doubt, then, this gang will also be chasing the parts you have. You're going to need to take great care, Charles, and another thing ...'

'Tsssss...'.

The two men looked at each other and Perinne's heart started to beat hard, but then she saw the door to her right burst open and a boy walked in.

'Edmund!' Sir Charles's face reddened. 'You know never to come into my room without knocking.'

Perinne was now shaking but didn't want to move.

'I'll leave now, Charles. Keep me updated.'

'Er, yes, I will, er, sorry about the interruption.' Perinne watched as the stranger stood up, shook hands with her uncle and left by the just-opened door. Then her mouth dropped open and her eyes were wide with astonishment as her uncle shouted at the boy, raised his hand and hit him.

## Chapter 6

# A find on the marsh

James Clarke lifted the latch on the door of his cottage and walked in. The house was quiet, apart from the rhythmic clunking of the clock pendulum and the gentle snoring of his father-in-law who was sitting in a chair by the fire, which was burning low in the grate.

Hannah, seeing her husband approaching, put down her stitching and stood up. 'Oh, hello James, you're early; I thought you were Danny coming in.'

James went over to his wife and kissed her cheek. 'Yes, Sir Charles let me home early and I don't need to go there tomorrow, plus I have a surprise!' he said, taking off his woollen coat and rummaging in its pockets. He smiled broadly as he handed the purse to Hannah.

Hannah tipped three guinea coins into her palm and looked at her husband, puzzled.

'You don't look very excited,' James said.

'Yes, of course I am, it's just...'.

'What's wrong? Has something happened?'

'Daddy!' Sarah burst into the room and leapt at her father.

'And how's my little angel?' James lifted his daughter and swung her around as she giggled. He looked back to Hannah. 'Has something happened, Hannah?'

'Daddy, Jack's been fighting and Danny came home late!' Sarah cut in.

'What?' James put Sarah gently down on the floor.

'Sarah!' Hannah shouted.

'Well, Hannah?'

'Edmund Tarrant attacked me.' Jack, having heard his father arrive, appeared at the doorway at the back of the room. His cheek had a small red cut and one of his eyes had bruising above it.

Grandpa had woken and was listening. 'Fighting? Where?'

'He started it,' Jack said and began to relate the events of the night before but was interrupted by Danny's voice, shouting from the kitchen.

'I'm back! I've got the fish, can I go out now?'

'No! Come in here, Daniel!'

'Father?' Danny thought, and 'Daniel'? That usually spelled trouble! Danny saw the room was filled with his family. He went in and stood next to Jack who looked down at Danny, pressing his lips together.

'I hear you were late home last night?' James Clarke looked directly at his youngest son and pointed to a wooden stool next to the fire. Danny sat down on the stool which was next to Grandpa who put his unlit pipe into his mouth and winked at him.

'Taken with John's old tales again? You don't think about what your mother's feeling? And the Forest at night is *not* a place for young lads out alone!' Danny saw his father's forehead wrinkle as his eyebrows formed a deep frown. Danny said nothing.

James turned back to his eldest son. 'Now, this fight, Jack?'

As his father moved towards a chair and sat down, Jack continued his tale.

'But why would I be shooting? I don't have a gun.' He paused thinking of what Danny had said last night. 'Edmund Tarrant probably has though, hasn't he? Maybe it was him, and his rich friends!'

'Quiet!' James Clarke's face reddened. 'What else did you see?'

'Nothing, just the men, running, I think there was a cart too!'

'And what were they like?'

'It was dark, just men, father, I didn't see much of them!'

'Think, boy, think!' James Clarke banged his fist on the table.

Grandpa jumped and Sarah started to cry. Hannah picked her up onto her lap, gently pulling her head to her chest and kissing her curly hair. 'Shhh ...'.

James Clarke took a deep breath. 'That's it! You are both forbidden to go near the marsh, do you understand? There are plenty of other places to go to with your friends. And you, Danny, you're not to go to Uncle John's house until I say you can, and don't let me find you've disobeyed me.'

'Yes, father,' Jack said, holding his head down.

'But why can't I go to the marsh?' Danny was stunned. 'It was our Jack who got into the fight, not me!'

James leapt to his feet, almost knocking his chair to the floor. 'You'll do as I say and not question me!' He took another deep breath and then exhaled a huge sigh. 'Now Jack, you get to your room, you look like you need to rest. Danny, you'll do chores.'

'But I've just been to town and done chores this morning!'

'Don't make things worse for yourself! Go and work the ground in the garden, there'll be things to plant soon. GO!'

Danny jumped off the stool and ran into the back of the house. Jack made his weary way back up the stairs.

'They only be doin' lads' stuff, James,' Grandpa said, leaning over to knock the ashes from his dead pipe.

'They were both in danger!' said James. 'Let's have

some ale, Hannah please.' He sat down at the table and put his head in his hands.

Will Gibbs rummaged through the wooden crate holding his father's old hunting things and found some rope. He took his knife and cut a length. 'Here, Sam.'

The dog ran over wagging his long tail, his tongue hanging from the side of his mouth. Will wound the rope around the dog's neck and made a knot, gently pulling it to make sure it didn't slip. Sam shook his head; he wasn't used to being tethered.

'What's going on with the dog?' Beth, who was wearing a pale blue linen dress with an apron, came in through the door and laughed at Sam, who was still trying to shake off the rope.

'Just goin' on the 'arbour,' Will replied.

'But why the rope? Sam's been out with you plenty and come to no harm,' Beth said, rubbing the dog's head.

'Thought I might pull up onto the marsh, there'll be nestin' birds; don't want 'im runnin' all o'er 'em.'

'He'd sniff 'em out.'

Will smiled. 'You out workin' again t'night?'

'Aye, and let's hope it's a bit quieter tonight, a right rowdy lot there were last night,' Beth said, picking up a bucket.

'Is the water all gone again? I only fetched a bucketful this mornin',' Will said, feeling another task coming on. Beth looked and smiled, and Will took the bucket.

'Take that off Sam's neck. I'll be back in a while.'

Will walked up the lane towards the Bargate where there was a water pump. The familiar figure of old Isaac was standing near the pump talking to a weasel-like, bent-looking man he'd never seen before. The man was as pale as a ghost with thick, white side whiskers down to his chin. He wore a dark, woollen coat and a round hat with buckle on a band around it. His shoes also had buckles. He was holding the reins of a dapple-coated horse, which was helping itself to a drink from the adjacent trough. Another man dressed much plainer, who he had seen now and then in the town, was also in the group. At first they didn't hear Will approaching.

'Fifty ankers, off the *Helena* and into th'harbour. We fetched some silks too, which should fetch a fair price, and ...' Isaac stopped as he heard the crunch of Will's boots.

'Here's a good lad,' he laughed smacking Will on the back. Will recoiled, Isaac may have been sober for once, but his breath stank of stale ale and tobacco. He wasn't wearing his ridiculous clothes of the night before but had a brown woollen coat and a felt hat.

The two other men looked at each other. 'We'll be off now and meet tonight at the Eight Bells,' the weasel said and he lifted his foot into a stirrup and launched himself awkwardly onto his horse's back and rode off. The familiar man looked at Will, nodded at Isaac and walked off towards the High Street.

Will began pumping water into the bucket.

'Your mother's a beautiful woman, Will lad; she won't turn me down forever ye know,' Isaac said, smiling.

Will didn't answer. 'Not if I can help it,' he thought. He groaned as he picked up the heavy bucket and began walking back to the house, trying not to let any water slop over the brim. He half expected Isaac to walk with him and continue the one-sided conversation, but, instead, he strode off towards the High Street.

The rope now in his coat pocket, Will whistled for Sam who came bounding into the small yard from wherever he'd been sniffing around. 'Come on boy, let's go.' Will popped his head into the back room, but there was no one there to say goodbye to, so the dog and boy set out. The little boat was tied where Will had left it the night before. The river was high due to the rain over the past week, but the tide was on the ebb. Although a little behind time, Will should reach the marsh at low tide and hopefully find some evidence from last night. Sam stood at the front of the boat the light breeze blowing through his white coat and his long, brown ears. Soon they'd rowed under the bridge and passed the Priory and the Wharf. Here boats were tied up and people were mending, fixing and carrying goods to and fro. A man with a cart was shouting.

To his left the reed beds of the marsh began to appear. They were old and faded after the winter and would soon be replaced by the new shoots of spring. Will had no idea where to set down but thought it best to get as close to the mouth of the channel that was used to approach the Ship in Distress, as this was a popular channel with smugglers. He soon saw the white gravel of the marsh's bank. After rowing towards the shore he jumped out of the boat and dragged it onto the land. Sam had stayed aboard and Will took the rope and tied it gently around the dog's neck.

'Now, sniffing Sam, let's see if ye can follow a trail!'

The two wandered about the water's edge and explored the creeks. Will wasn't sure what he was looking for. There were a few other people, some fishing with line and hook and others who seemed simply to be walking around. New Forest ponies wandered on the marsh and huge flocks of birds waded in the shallows, trilling and chattering.

Will looked up at the clouds that were gathering, darkening as they thickened. A cold wind had begun to blow from inland and Will thought he would start back. There was no sign of the kid from this morning who'd said he'd meet him, but Will didn't care. All he'd done was confirmed something had happened here last night. It had made him laugh when the boy fell over.

A mallard duck took off, the sudden burst of flapping making Will jump and drop the rope. Sam, feeling his freedom, ran off.

'Sam, Sam, come 'ere! Come back! Sam!'

The dog splashed into the reed bed and a flutter of birds burst into the sky. Will trod over the boggy ground to try to catch him when suddenly something caught his eye. A small wooden box was bobbing along in the ripples being made by Sam. Treading carefully, Will stretched out for the box. It was just out of reach. He looked around for something to use and snapped a reed. Sam came bounding back again, making more waves and sending the box just out of Will's reach. 'Sit, Sam!' The dog wandered away as Will stretched out once again, this time almost losing his balance. He prodded around the box with the old reed to motion the box his way. Soon his patience was rewarded and the box began to float towards him.

It wasn't very big, just a square with each side six or seven inches. As he lifted it, water dribbled off, so it was sealed somehow. It wasn't heavy. He gave it a shake and it made a noise as though filled with nails, or glass marbles. The words *M Costelot, Privé* and *Treize* were burned into one of the sides. 'What does it mean?' Will asked himself.

His feet were sinking into the brown sludge of the water's edge. He lifted them out and made his way to the dry bank. Sam bounded back and shook himself, showering Will with salty water. His boots were now wet and his feet cold and he decided to get back home and open the box there.

41

Beth Gibbs had been to the High Street to look at some fabrics. She wanted to make a new dress and although she'd saved enough from her wages to buy some linen, she'd not found what she wanted. She approached the house from the back door. Will's boots were outside and were damp and covered in mud. Opening the door she found Will seated at the table trying to open a wooden box with a knife.

'What've you there?'

'Found it on the marsh.' He shook it. 'Don't know what's inside.'

Beth took off her coat and hung it on the back of the door. 'Why'd ye go to the marsh, Will?'

Will looked up. 'Why?'

'What made you go to the marsh today?' Beth repeated.

'Don't tell Mother but I 'eard shots last night. Some kid this mornin' told me 'is brother'd seen somethin', so thought I'd go and look, that's all. Why'd you ask?'

'The fuss in the George last night, they were on about the marsh.'

'Smugglers, I thought,' Will put the box down.

'I don't think it's smugglers, Will. Somethin' else's going on.'

## Chapter 7

# A surprise for Perinne

'Miss?'

Perinne gasped as she turned but let out her breath in relief as she recognised Lucy, the maid from earlier.

'I, I am lost,' said Perinne.

'Let's go to your room,' said Lucy. 'We need to get you ready for dinner.'

In the library Edmund was now sitting in the leather chair. He had short, thick brown hair and a square face. His large, grey-green eyes were wide in anticipation. Sir Charles glared at him, furious.

'What do you think you are doing bursting in like that?'

'I'm sorry, father.' Edmund played with his hands on his lap. 'I just wanted to tell you the pony has arrived.'

'Just make sure you never do that again or your punishment will be harsher, do you understand? Now go, it must be time for dinner.'

Edmund jumped out of the chair and left the room as quickly as he could. When he'd closed the door, Sir

Charles walked over to his desk and kicked the chair away. He picked up a pile of papers and put them into the desk drawer. He closed the drawer with a slam, locked it and put the key into his waistcoat pocket.

'Do I have to go to dinner?' Perinne asked as she watched Lucy unpack the rest of the clothes from the trunk and store them in drawers in the dresser.

Lucy picked up one of the dresses Perinne had thrown onto the bed earlier and held it up. It was yellow with a high collar and long sleeves with lace at the cuffs.

'Will you wear this now?'

Perinne shook her head, she was quite happy with the plain dress she was wearing.

'The mistress is expecting you, she wants to meet you, miss.'

Perinne shrugged.

'Come on, miss, I'll take you to the dining room; don't want you gettin' lost again, do we?' Lucy walked over to open the door and smiled. 'Susan's cooking isn't that bad!'

The dining room of Cliff House was a corner room on the ground floor and was painted in a pale blue. Two large windows rose from floor to ceiling and overlooked the grounds. The sun that earlier had been pouring into Perinne's room had been replaced by grey clouds and a fire had been set in the fireplace. The fire surround was beautifully carved showing hounds chasing hares.

Hello, darling.' Jane Menniere was sitting at the centre of the table directly across from a pale, slim-faced woman wearing a dark red gown and lace cap. She was small and despite being seated looked bony.

'Perinne, this is Lady Elizabeth, Uncle Charles's wife. She has agreed that you may call her Aunt.'

Perinne gave a little curtsey but said nothing and she wondered if Uncle Charles hit her sometimes as he'd just hit Edmund. A place had been set to her mother's right and Perinne sat down.

Soon Edmund appeared and drew back the chair opposite Perinne. Sir Charles had settled at the head of the long table, around which Perinne thought fifteen to twenty people could easily fit. The table was set with a white linen cloth. Five china plates with knives, forks and spoons were in position, as were several glasses.

Servants arrived with bowls of soup, plates of meat and bread, along with some cheeses, salads and vegetables. One of them was Lucy who had changed aprons and wore a different cap. A plate with sugarplums was placed between Perinne and Edmund and Lucy poured a glass of wine for Sir Charles. As Lucy leaned across, obscuring Sir Charles's view, Edmund smirked at Perinne.

'So, Perinne,' Uncle Charles began, 'I hope you are rested after your journey?'

Perinne looked at Lucy, who looked up at the ceiling.

'Yes, thank you Uncle.'

'Good, because I have a surprise for you, though it will have to wait until after our meal!' His round face smiled widely.

Perinne smiled back. She couldn't think what it could be, but she had seen Edmund purse his lips. He obviously knew what it was about.

The dinner passed quietly with Jane talking about the journey and saying how she didn't think Christchurch had changed much since her last visit a long time ago. Perinne had never heard her maman mention Christchurch before and wondered if she'd made it up for something to say.

As the servants took away the last of the plates Edmund stood up, pushing back his chair. 'May we go now, father?'

Sir Charles nodded. 'Well, let's get our coats. Are you ready for your surprise, Perinne?'

The afternoon had grown cold. Aunt Elizabeth decided to stay indoors, but Perinne, Edmund, Uncle Charles and Jane made their way through the house to the rear, through a courtyard and across to some stables. Perinne recognised the four coach horses that were now comfortable in their stalls. Next to these stood a taller black horse, but, peeking out from another stall was a pony. The group followed Sir Charles who had now opened the stall door.

'Here you are, Perinne, your own Forrester pony.'

Perinne's pretty hazel eyes were like saucers. She loved to ride, but she'd had to leave her own horse at home in France. She walked across the straw bed to the little pony, its nose sniffing towards her as she stroked his fair mane which was falling softly onto its chestnut brown coat.

'For *me*? What is his name?'

Sir Charles smiled. 'He doesn't have one, you must choose.'

'May we saddle them up, father?' Edmund had pushed through to the stall where Perinne was now stroking the nose of the little pony.

'Yes, but don't go far, there isn't much left of the light and it looks as though we'll get rain soon.' And with that Sir Charles strode out of the stables.

A stable boy appeared and saddled up the horses. Perinne was helped up onto her new pony.

'Take care, and stay with Edmund.' Jane Menniere waved as her daughter and Edmund Tarrant rode out to the gates.

Perinne and the little pony soon got used to each other, but she couldn't keep up with Edmund who kept riding off.

'Come on, get a move on!' he shouted back at them once again.

Further along, a branch from a tree swung back and would have caught Perinne's face had she not ducked out of the way in time. She was sure Edmund had let go of it deliberately before he sped off again. Edmund had now reached the cliff top and Perinne caught up with him. The wind was in her face and the air smelled salty. Gulls squawked overhead and she could hear waves crashing on the beach below.

'Where is that?' she said, pointing to the white stacks. 'I saw them from the ship and I can see them from my room.'

'They're called the Needles and that's the Isle of Wight, stupid,' scoffed Edmund. 'Over there is Muddiford, don't you recognise it? You would've passed by the Haven Inn on your way into the harbour.' And at that he turned around and galloped off.

Perrine carried on along the cliff top towards the harbour. In the distance, she could make out the Priory church high above the other buildings. 'It is Sunday tomorrow, I expect we shall go to church,' she said to herself. She leaned down and patted the neck of the pony.

'I need a name for you, do I not, boy?'

She looked across the sea, the horizon now lost in misty greyness, and thought about her home in Rennes. She thought about her horse there, Orion. He would be looked after by her father and by Pierre, one of the stable hands who had taught Perinne to ride. 'Pierre. Yes that would be a good name for you. I shall call you Pierre.'

She gently nudged him with her heels and set off back to Cliff House the way she had come, glad that there was no sight of Edmund. It would be getting dark soon.

When Lucy opened the shutters on the window of Perinne's bedroom the next morning the air smelled damp. It had rained heavily in the night and was still drizzling. At supper the night before she had heard that the family would indeed attend church and Perinne was now back in the Tarrant's coach on the way to the Priory.

Also that morning, in Christchurch, Will Gibbs was lighting the fire. Meg was up in the room above, singing.

'Mother sounds happy,' said Will to Beth who was eating bread she'd brought back from the George the night before.

'She's got a new man,' laughed Beth. 'Well she hopes she has!'

Will stopped prodding the fire and looked at his sister. 'Please tell me it isn't Isaac!'

'No, she wasn't that drunk!'

'Who then?'

'A grocer from down the Purewell.'

Will tutted and carried on poking at the fire.

'She wants us to go to church; appears he'll be there. She wants him to think us Godly folks!'

Danny was tugging at his best boots. They were getting tight, but until Jack needed new ones he would have to put up with them. Sunday meant that they had to go to church. Although it only took Danny half an hour, they needed longer to walk to Christchurch with Sarah coming along. It was cold and he hoped that the drizzle would stop. The last thing he wanted was to sit in the damp for an hour listening to Reverend Jackson.

When Danny and his family arrived at the church the sun was breaking through the clouds again and the bells were ringing. As they passed through the door he wondered where they'd be able to sit. The boxed pews for the town's dignitaries were at the front and the rows behind were filling. Danny's family made their way to one of the pews and sat down. Danny stared up at the towering arches and the ornately painted wooden beams of the roof. Townsfolk were also coming in and soon the building was echoing with people's voices. Sarah's teeth were chattering in the chill and she snuggled between her parents. Danny and Jack moved closer to each other to try to keep warm. Although it wasn't dark outside, candles flickered at the altar and in the pulpit. A musky smell hung in the air.

A church warden walked down the central aisle and asked the people on the benches to stand. Danny turned to see a procession of choir boys led by the sexton. The vicar appeared next and then Sir Charles Tarrant with Lady Elizabeth, Edmund and the woman and girl who had arrived on the launch the day before. As Danny watched them walk by, he caught sight of Will, who was standing in the north aisle behind the pillars. Jack nudged Danny and nodded towards Edmund who sneered as he passed by the boys. The girl, seeing Edmund's expression, also turned and looked at Danny, then carried on.

The service was long and Danny was bored so it was a relief when the vicar finished and led the local dignitaries back up the aisle and out of the Priory. The clouds had cleared and the sky was glowing with reds and golds of the early evening sun. The vicar was talking to Sir Charles as Danny walked through the porch, straggling behind his family in hope of seeing Will. He was in luck.

'Hello, again,' he looked up at Will, who was standing with an attractive older girl. Will smiled. 'This is my sister, Beth, I saw thee with yer family,' he said, nodding towards the pathway where the Clarkes were walking towards the gate.

Danny cocked his head to one side and Will leaned down.

'Did you go to the marsh yesterday?' asked Danny.

'Aye, for a short while,' Will replied.

Danny looked from side to side and behind him and cupped his hand to his mouth. 'Did you find anything?'

'Might've done,' Will teased. 'Anyway, where were ye?'

'In trouble, and father has forbidden me to go to the marsh, but I could do, he wouldn't find out.'

Danny's family were now talking to another family who were with a boy from Danny's school.

'Meet me tomorrow,' said Will.

'I've got school tomorrow,' Danny frowned, 'but I can say I feel unwell and come away!'

'Nay, ye'll end up in e'en more trouble. I've to work in any case. Can ye meet me about 4 o'clock?'

'Yes, how about Muddiford? I can go there.'

Will smiled, 'Muddiford, tis then, see ye there!'

'Danny!' James Clarke was waving for his son to come to him.

'See you there!' Excited, Danny ran to his family.

Perinne had been standing next to her mother while Sir Charles had introduced them to the vicar. She was watching one of the boys that Edmund had pulled a face at on the way into church. He was with a taller, dark-haired boy who wasn't very well dressed for church. 'I wonder what they are up to,' she thought.

## Chapter 8

# Who will share the mystery?

'You're quiet.' Jack broke the silence.

Danny shrugged. 'This rotten weather, that's all.'

'It's never bothered you before,' Jack laughed. 'Anyway, who was that you were talking to after church yesterday?'

'No one.'

Jack and Danny were making their way back home from school, the skies were grey but it had stopped raining and the road was full of puddles.

'Come on, who was it? I haven't seen him before.'

'Why ask me now and not yesterday?'

'Just thought about it.'

'Just someone I met, that's all.'

Before Jack could press him further the drumming of hooves broke the silence and two horses thundered past, splashing muddy water over Danny and Jack, soaking and dirtying their stockings. It was Edmund Tarrant with one of his friends; they both looked back at the pair, laughing.

'I'm going to kill that cod's head one day!' Danny yelled after the horses that had now disappeared.

'Don't let father hear you saying things like that!' Jack teasingly poked his brother's arm. 'You'll end up banned from going anywhere! Who talks like that - this new friend of yours?'

Danny ignored his question and started running. 'Race you!'

'Hey, wait!'

When the boys arrived home the skies had begun to clear and after his chores Danny set out for Muddiford.

Will had been up since first light. He'd been out fishing and had nets to mend on his return. He was hungry, but there hadn't been anything in the house when he got home. He whistled for Sam and took a penny from a purse in the drawer of the old dresser and set out. He hadn't decided whether to tell Danny about the box he'd found on the marsh. He hadn't tried to open it again since he first got it home and had hidden it amongst his few things stored behind his bed. He walked along the High Street with Sam at his side and despite it being late in the day could smell bread baking in Mr Tizzard's bakery; he called in and bought some to eat along the way.

The day's rain had stopped and the townsfolk were out and about. Women lifted their skirts to avoid the puddles, small children shrilled as they jumped in and out of them. A cart was slowly rattling along in the ruts of the road, carrying barrels from one of the breweries. Will reached the end of the street and turned past the town hall in time to see a coach pulling out of the George. He slipped in through the archway to look if Beth were about but couldn't see her. There were men sitting drinking beer and smoking pipes. A dog growled at Sam and Will. As he turned to leave he could hear arguing and saw that one of the men was the familiar one he'd seen with Isaac by the water pump; this must be where he'd seen him before.

Danny could see the tall shape of Will approaching with a dog happily scampering at his heels. He waved and Will waved back. The afternoon was chilly from a northerly wind and the boys decided to walk along the beach to keep warm.

'Can't have a dog,' Danny said, leaning down to rub Sam's head. 'Father says they belong on farms, working. He says they take too much feeding and steal food from children.'

'He followed me father 'ome one night, he were limpin' and he hung around,' replied Will. He picked up a stick and threw it into the sea and Sam chased after it, splashing happily in the waves. 'Father were going to 'ave 'im killed, but he turned out to be a good rabbit catcher. He lives off the waste food me sister brings from the George.'

In the bay ships with billowing sails could be seen, oars from the oar ports sticking out like bristles on a brush. Smaller boats seemed to appear and disappear as they rose and fell on the choppy grey sea. The sun was low in the west now, its pale yellow glow lighting up the Needles rocks.

'What does your father do?' Danny asked.

'He's dead.' Will bowed his head down towards Sam, who'd returned the stick and had dropped it at his feet.

'Sorry,' Danny looked at him, 'Then how do you live?'

'I work for Master Hardyman. I help 'im on the *Solomon* and I mend nets. Ye must know that, ye nearly ruined a mornin's work when you tripped over 'em! Beth works at the George in town and Mother sews stockin's at home. I 'ave two older sisters, they're both married and have gone away, we don't see 'em. I saw thy family yesterday. Did ye say yer father works at Tarrant's place?'

'Yes. I'm not sure what he does. He has to go away a lot.' It seemed unfair that Will had to work so hard and he couldn't think what life would be like if his own father wasn't around. Danny was deep in thought as the pair continued along the beach where holm oak trees provided a woody backdrop. Then a pathway behind the golden sands began to slope gently upwards. More trees grew here and were only a few feet above the beach where the boys decided to sit down under the cliffs, sheltered from the wind. Sam curled himself by Will's legs.

Perinne was pleased that she didn't have to ride with Edmund. The more she was with him, the more she disliked him. He was, well, just so stupid. She was glad to be out of Cliff House too. Everyone seemed to be fussing about her. The maid was all right though. She was only doing as she was ordered. She hadn't said anything about finding her at the door of the library. The little pony made his way through the trees towards the cliff top. The salt air was different from the smells of the French countryside. As she approached the edge of the copse she noticed two figures below on the beach. It was the two boys she'd seen yesterday. The taller one was throwing a stick into the sea. Perinne watched as the boys chatted intently. Then they began to walk towards her. She backed Pierre behind a tree, but they didn't look up. She inched forward curiously and looked over the edge. She could hear the boys talking a few feet below.

'So, what do you think's going on?' Danny started.

Will shrugged. 'Probably just smugglers, I s'pose. A lot of 'em 'ave hand pistols.'

'Do they? How do you know?'

Will took a moment to respond. 'Beth hears talk in the George.'

'My brother Jack says if the smugglers catch you at night they kidnap you and take you off on their ships!'

Will laughed out loud. 'Don't be daft, nearly *everyone* in Christchurch is a smuggler, or at least takes in the spoils. Though I'd still keep clear of 'em goin' about their business! Them ships now,' Will pointed. 'They're probably bringin' in tea and brandy; watch, they'll of'en stop an' the tub boats will side up an' lift off contraband, e'en in broad daylight. Ridin' officers turn a blind eye most the time.'

'So if it's for townspeople why take the stuff further away on carts?' Danny asked.

'Depends what's come in,' Will answered. 'The carts'll do a run from here out to inns 'cross the Forest and Bourne Heath, 'specially brandy. It's all organised.'

'But ... .' Will started as stones tumbled down the edge of the cliff. Sam stirred from his sleep and the boys looked up but could see nothing there.

'But,' Will continued, 'I don't think they were smugglers as we know 'em.'

'Why?'

'The shots, for a start, there might be shootin' on the beach if the ridin' officers are waitin', but they don't of'en get followed into the harbour.'

'The cart I saw made a real racket thundering along. Why was it going to Winchester?'

'Takin' goods I expect, but somethin' different's 'appening. Local carts are muffled ye know, some farmers put leather on the horse shoes and have muffled harnesses to keep as quiet as possible.'

'Then, what about our mystery? What do we know?' Danny pressed.

'First, your brother were attacked.'

'Yes, Edmund Tarrant was there, he could have something to do with it!' Danny interrupted.

Will continued. 'Your Jack 'eard shots, I 'eard shots and saw a boat dashin' away. You saw the cart goin' straight to Winchester and our Beth says somethin's goin' on, and she's usually right!'

Another rumble of stones showered onto the boys and a pony whinnied. Sam started to bark up at the cliff top. Turning quickly they saw a girl on a pony above them wearing a brown cloak which hung over the pony's back. Her long black hair, which was trailing from underneath a woollen bonnet, was blowing in the breeze.

'Hey! You!' Danny shouted. He jumped to his feet. Will stood too.

'What is it you are talking about?' the girl called down.

'What's it to do with you!' Danny shouted back.

'It's the girl from the boat who were at church with the Tarrants,' Will whispered.

The girl started to ride along the shallow cliff edge down to where she could join the beach.

'Say nothing, Will, she's a Tarrant!'

'She sounds French,' Will added.

Danny looked at Will in surprise. 'How does he know these things?' he thought to himself.

Sand scattered as the little chestnut pony made its way towards them. Sam had stopped barking and was hanging around Will's legs.

'Hello, I saw both of you at the church yesterday.'

'Yes, we saw you, with Edmund Tarrant.' Danny pulled a face as he said the name.

'I was with my maman,' replied Perinne. 'I had no choice but to be with him. It does not mean that I like him though.'

Now that she was close to him, Will could see that whilst Perinne had a plain face, her tanned skin made her look healthy, and she was quite pretty.

'Where're ye from then?' he asked her.

'Rennes, it is in France,' she replied and pointed out to sea.

Danny and Will sat down again. Perinne jumped off the pony and stood by it, stroking its mane.

'You have a mystery?' she asked.

'Go away,' Danny said.

'We were talkin' 'bout smugglers,' Will cut in. Danny shot him a glance.

'Why?' Perinne asked.

'Danny knows nothin', I was tellin' him about their ways. Some of the stuff comes from France. Like brandy.' Will said.

'But why is it necessary for it to be smuggled?' asked Perinne as she tied the pony's reins to a tree.

'To avoid payin' duty.' Will explained. 'Duty makes goods from abroad expensive. There's money to be made bringin' things in without the customs makin' their charges. Folks make nothin' on the land and not much more from the sea. Keeps some folk alive it does, smugglin'.'

Perinne sat down on the sand and stroked Sam, who rolled onto his back, enjoying the attention. Danny made circles in the sand with his finger.

'You do not like me?' Perinne said.

'How can we trust you? We've only just met you and you are living with the Tarrants!'

'You think your mystery is to do with Edmund?' Perinne asked.

The boys looked at each other.

'I think that you are wrong,' she added.

'Why's that then?' Danny scoffed and nudged Will, winking at him.

'Because I think I know what your mystery is.'

58

'Well, are you going to tell us then?' pressed Danny.

Perinne got up and went over to the pony, unhitching the reins. She put her foot into the stirrup and hoisted herself onto the pony's back, just like a boy.

'You have told me to go away,' she replied, pulling on the reins.

'Wait! Tell us why Edmund isn't involved,' Danny pleaded.

'Let her go, Danny,' Will tugged on Danny's sleeve, but Danny shook him off and made towards Perinne.

'Go on, tell us and we'll let you know what we were talking about.'

Will shook his head.

'I did not say that he was not involved, just that the mystery may not be to do with him.'

'Please tell us, er, what's your name?'

'My name is Perinne.'

'Please, Perinne, tell us, and we'll let you help us solve the mystery,' Danny begged.

'Maybe it is you who can help me to solve it,' Perinne teased. 'Meet me here again at the same time tomorrow and I will think about whether I shall tell you.' And at that Perinne turned the little pony and rode away.

'Do you really think she knows something, Will?'

'Maybe,' Will replied. 'She's livin' at Cliff House, per'aps she's 'eard somethin'. Let's meet again tomorrow, see if she turns up.'

'Will we tell her our side?' Danny asked.

'We'll see.'

## Chapter 9

# A stranger in the George

The evening brought wild gales and heavy rain to Christchurch. Two men were sitting in a dark, low-ceilinged room. The noise of the wind whistled through the eaves and a small window rattled. One of the men was sitting on the edge of a low cot bed. His long hair was untidy, his face marked by the pox. His clothes were ill-fitting and his stockings had holes in them. The other man was better dressed and his light brown hair was neatly tied. He was seated on a stool by a table. A nearby oil lamp remained unlit and a single candle gave an eerie glow. They each held a tankard of ale.

'Ye need to lay low, Tom, they'll know ye'll head back here.'

'Landlord won't want me 'ere either, if he knew,' Tom replied.

'P'raps ye should have stayed in the Forest longer.' Adam Litty drank his tankard empty.

'Got to sort you lot out, haven't I?' Tom Pike took a swig and wiped his whiskery chin on the sleeve of his grubby shirt. 'So they were layin' in wait then? How much of the load did they get?'

''Bout 'alf.'

'And Ginn, what does he think on it?'

'He were furious, but we weren't expectin' it in for

another week. Pity we couldn't get you out in time to sort it. He says we'd 'ave got all thirteen 'ad you'd been there, but we've only six. He says you're the best plotter he's ever known.'

'Come on, Adam, the men could've handled it if ye'd had time. Tarrant's men were lucky! And we were lucky no one got shot. That's the bother o' gettin' involved with the likes of Meekwick Ginn. Where's the wench with the grub?'

Adam Litty got up, taking care not to catch his head on the low beams. He walked to the door and peered out. 'Beth! Where's our food?' His gruff voice bellowed down the narrow wooden staircase.

Tom banged his tankard onto the table. 'Ask 'er for more ale.'

There was no reply, but he could hear Adam talking. It was Ginn, he was here.

Meekwick Ginn pushed open the door and doddered over towards the table. Tom jumped up and held out his hand, but Ginn ignored it.

'How much is this costing me?' Ginn snarled, his pale face ghost-like as he peered around the dim, candle-lit room. His black coat twisted on his bent back. He leaned on his stick.

'It's just for t'night,' Tom replied, sitting back on the bed.

'They'd go lookin' for him at 'ome, and we didn't know who to trust at the Ship,' Adam said, coming in through the door and holding it open for Beth. She was carrying a tray with a plate of fish and vegetables, and two tankards of ale.

'Fetch ale for the gentleman, will ye Beth,' Adam said and dipped his hand in his pocket for a few coins.

'Brandy,' Ginn growled, 'and some of that fish.' Adam nodded to Beth who picked up the men's empty tankards and left.

Ginn put his hand to his back and sat down next to Tom, smacking him between the shoulders. Tom coughed.

'Prison's done you no good, then Pike, but you're out now and you're back here working for me 'till we get this sorted.'

He looked at Tom and Adam in turn, his brow frowning and face serious. 'Now, I expect Tarrant's got the boxes we want stashed away at Cliff House. I've a man working there and he's trying to find out where. Once we know, I want you and your men to break in and get them for me.'

Tom, who had started to eat the food, stopped chewing. He pulled a fish bone from the corner of his mouth, then shook his head. 'Won't be easy that, Mr Ginn, may take some time.'

There was a knock on the door and Beth walked in with another plate of food and a glass of brandy. She put it on the table and turned towards the door.

'What's in the boxes then?' Tom asked.

'Quiet!' Ginn glared at him fiercely.

Adam Litty nodded at Beth who left quickly, closing the door behind her.

'Keep that damned tongue still. I hope prison hasn't dulled your wits, we need to keep this between ourselves,' Ginn growled, staring menacingly at Tom. 'Landlord here's not to be trusted. Why did you bring him here, Litty?'

'Too many o' Tarrant's men go to the Ship and they said they'd done enough for us at the Eight Bells. It was better here, so I said I needed a room for a visitor. They're happy to take the money. Besides landlord don't seem to know about the job.' Adam tugged at his collar, he was sweating now.

'I hope not. Now, tell me, our stuff's moved on from the Eight Bells as instructed I hope?'

'Yes, Mr Ginn.'

'How many of your men know where the goods are

now?'

'Just me an' two others. They're the ones as fetched Tom here, trust 'em wi' me' life, I would.'

'I hope that's so.'

'But if this wet weather carries on, I'm not sure how long we can keep 'em hidden where they are.'

'I don't want them damaged. Tell Tom here all about it and then no one else, do you understand? Then wait until you hear from me about where Tarrant has the stuff. Tom, I need you to come up with a plan. I need all thirteen boxes or none of us will be paid!'

Ginn finished the plate of fish and knocked back his glass of brandy. He stood up and threw some coins onto the table.

'I'll be in touch.' And with that he grabbed his stick and stamped out of the room.

'Phew! Nasty piece o' work that one,' Adam said.

Tom lay back on the bed. 'What's in these boxes that need be kept so secret?'

'No idea.'

'Must be somethin' out the ord'nary for 'im to want to spring me out of gaol. And for Tarrant to have a crew on the job. Don't like the idea of breaking into Cliff House much.'

'Aye, Tom. But 'e's payin' well.'

'Strange affair though. Where's the stuff now then?'

Beth didn't know whether to go back into the room. The nasty weasel-like man had brushed past her without looking. She knew the others though. Adam Litty was a regular at the George and Tom Pike worked near Burton on the land. But he'd been caught with smuggled goods and had been sent to Winchester Gaol. That's what she'd heard.

Someone said it'd been in *The Journal*. His family nearly had to go to the poor house but for the farmer helping them by giving them work for food. And now he'd escaped! Mr Martin, the landlord, would be in real trouble if an escaped prisoner were found here in the George. She'd leave the plate for the morning maids to clear away.

When she arrived home there was a light burning in the window. She expected mother and Will to be in bed by now. She kept warning them about leaving a candle, these cottages easily caught fire.

After snuffing it out, she climbed the steps into the attic room. Her mother was sound asleep. She pulled across the drape that was dividing the room to see Will asleep too. She knew he had to be up early in the morning but gently shook his shoulder. 'Brother,' she whispered.

'Mmm, Beth? What's wrong?'

'Shhh!' Beth pressed her finger gently on Will's lips and continued in a whisper, 'some men in the George were talking about boxes! I think they may have something to do with what's going on?'

Will sat up, the room was pitch-black, and he could smell stale ale and tobacco on his sister's clothes. 'Did ye know 'em ?'

'One was Adam Litty and the other Tom Pike.'

'Not sure I know Litty, and it couldn't have been Tom Pike, he's in gaol!'

'Not now he isn't! And there was another man, horrible he was. The others seemed scared of him.'

'Tom Pike scared of someone! Are you sure?'

'Yes, I've never seen the man before. He looked really strange, bent back and pale as you'd never believe.'

'Sounds like the man I saw with Isaac t'other day.'

'Isaac?'

It was Will's turn to say 'shhh'. 'Let's talk about this tomorrow. I've got to be up in a few hours.'

## Chapter 10

# A clash on the beach

When Danny arrived back from school the next day his father was home. He could see him through the small window as he approached the cottage. He was sitting writing. Danny lifted the latch of the back door as quietly as he could. He didn't want to have to do chores or worse, run errands. He wanted to meet up with Will. But the day was blustery after the storms of the night before and the wind rushed past him as he opened the door.

'Hello, Danny. Hope you've worked hard at school today,' James Clarke said. He dipped his quill pen into the inkpot and continued his work. Danny sighed. On the table was a copy of the *Salisbury and Winchester Journal*. Father sometimes brought a copy home. Danny loved to look through it and see what had been happening.

'It was boring - arithmetic, then Latin.' He pulled the newspaper towards him, glancing at the stories. Then as he read on, he gasped.

'HAMPSHIRE - Prisoner Escapes Winchester Gaol – thought to be in hiding in the New Forest'.

'Is everything all right, Danny?'

Danny nodded, 'Yes, father.' He sat down and started to read.

*'At between three and five o'clock on Saturday morning*

*last, Christchurch farm hand, Tom Pike made his
escape from the gaol at Winchester. When he escaped
he made a daring climb of the walls and got away
with the help of unknown accomplices. It is believed
the villains hid him in a wagon waiting outside and
such a wagon was heard by several persons in the
early hours. Nearby, Doctor John Roots, returning
from visiting the sick, also heard the noise. The time
he reported on his watch showed the hour to be five
o'clock. At the same time wardens were making
their rounds. They discovered the man missing. They
called upon soldiers from the barracks to give chase.
Unfortunately the scoundrels had a head start and by
the words of the few witnesses headed away on the
Romsey Road.'*

'The smugglers!' Danny muttered under his breath.

James Clarke looked up. 'What is it Danny?'

'Nothing, father.'

'What are you reading?'

'There's an escaped prisoner hiding in the Forest.'

James laughed. 'You'd better stay away then or he may
kidnap you!'

'That's just a story, father,' Danny responded. He read
on. The story told how Tom Pike had been found with
*'several ankers of brandy, tea and various silks.'* He'd
been sent before the judge at the assizes in Winchester. He
was found guilty and sent to gaol. It said that he was lucky
not to have been sent to Newgate then on to Wapping to be
hung. Pike was, the newspaper said, *'driven to smuggling
to feed his large family... he was suspected of organising
smuggling gangs but nothing could be proven. This saved
him from a severe punishment.'* There was more about
smuggling and how it was now a big problem for the
authorities. Many soldiers were away fighting in America.
Extra customs and riding officers were being assigned for

the coast from Southampton to Poole.

Danny looked up to see his father finish writing. He saw him sprinkle sand from the small tin onto his work to dry the ink. James waited a few moments, tipped off the sand, then carefully folded the letter and walked over to the fireplace. Though the fire was usually kept burning at this time of the year, it was barely alight in the grate. Danny watched his father bend and light a taper from the embers, then use it to light a candle. He held his sealing wax to the flame and red liquid fell like a drop of blood onto the letter's fold. He pressed his seal to secure it.

'I'm going to walk into town to catch today's post chaise, Danny. Do you want to come?'

It was the last thing Danny wanted to do. 'May I go to meet my friends instead, Father?'

'Yes, but stay away from the marsh!'

As James Clarke left the room Danny caught sight of the letter. It was addressed to Sir George Cook. And the letter was being posted to London. Before he could see the whole address his father walked back into the room, wearing his warm, woollen coat and hat.

'Your mother's taken Grandpa to the barber, I'm meeting her there. Be good Danny and be home well before dark!'

Danny couldn't wait to tell Will about the escaped prisoner. It all fitted. The smugglers he'd seen may not have been smugglers at all. They must have been the men on the way to help Tom Pike escape! Danny grabbed his coat and set out for Muddiford. As he ran along the road he wondered what Tom Pike was like. Will had said yesterday that lots of people in Christchurch were smugglers. Were they? And this still didn't explain what had happened on the marsh.

Despite his father's warning, Danny decided they should go and take a look.

Will was standing at the water's edge when Danny arrived. Strands of hair were blowing about his face and he smelled of fish.

'Where's Sam?' Danny asked, looking around for the dog.

'Back at 'ome. I've been 'ere all mornin', master's been workin' off the shore today. I've been on the boat since dawn, sea's been rough. Have ye been to school today?'

'Yes. But something's happened, much more exciting.'

'Oh? What's that then?'

'I think I know why those men were off to Winchester.' Danny's chest rose with pride.

'Springin' Tom Pike from gaol?'

'How did *you* know? You see the *Journal* too?'

'Can't read. Well not enough for a whole piece in the paper.'

'So, *how*?' Danny was cross Will already knew the news. He wondered if he could trust his new friend. Then Will explained.

'Beth saw him with her own eyes. And she's been overhearing things again.'

As Danny looked at Will he saw Perinne riding along the shore on her pony. Seaweed washed up by the storms of the night before had piled onto the beach and was giving off a pungent smell. The water was splashing up as they approached.

'That girl's coming,' he said. 'Let's go before she gets here. I want to go to the marsh.'

'No,' Will replied gruffly. 'She knows something. We still don't know what's going on. Let's see if she'll tell us.'

'Hello again,' Perinne said, pulling at the reins. The pony stopped. Its hooves crunched on the pebbles that had replaced the sand of the shoreline. Will stroked the pony's forelock, taking his hand down its nose.

'What's 'is name?'

'Pierre,' Perinne replied.

Danny groaned.

'Have ye thought about whether ye'll 'elp us with our mystery?' Will asked.

She took a deep breath and looked over the sea. 'I am bored here,' she sighed. 'I will help if you will be my friend.'

'And Danny 'ere? Is he to be yer friend too?'

'I do not think he likes me, so maybe not.'

Will laughed and his eyes sparkled. 'Aye he does, he's just shy around young ladies.'

'No, I'm not!' Danny blushed.

'Well, let us agree to be friends and share our secrets about the mystery,' Perinne said, smiling.

Will held out his hand. 'Come on, Danny, let's all shake on it.'

Before they could seal their friendship a voice yelled out.

'Hey, you two ruffians, get away from her!'

The three turned to see Edmund Tarrant approaching with two other boys. They must have been hiding in the trees which backed onto the beach.

'Go home, Perinne, now!' Edmund demanded.

'No,' Perinne answered. 'They are my friends.'

'I'll tell father. Go, now!'

'No, I will not!'

'What were you talking about? Tell me!' Edmund grabbed the pony's bridle and pushed Will away. 'You stink.'

Will raised his hands ready for a fight.

Danny stepped forward. 'Get lost, cod's head!'

Edmund let go of the bridle and grabbed Danny by his coat. 'What did you call me, shorty? Such a foul tongue on you!'

'Leave him alone!' Will leapt forward.

'Adam, Simon, deal with him!' Edmund ordered.

A dark-haired boy jumped on Will and wrestled him to the ground. 'Come on, Adam, help me!' Simon yelled.

'Let go of me!' Danny kicked Edmund on the shin.

Edmund cried out in pain, pushing Danny so that they both fell onto the stony ground. Simon and Adam were now holding Will down. 'Stinky, stinky, stinky,' Simon goaded him, spitefully.

'Go home, Perinne!' Edmund growled.

'Non! Stop. Leave him alone!' Perinne shouted back.

Will yelped, winded, as Simon thumped him.

Perinne jumped off her pony. She threw herself onto the boys who were holding Will down, her cloak covering them. She began to hit out at them beating them with her fists. The two boys, surprised, tumbled off Will. Will rolled away, sprung to his feet and lunged at Edmund, pulling him off Danny.

Perinne scrambled to her feet and quickly ran between them. 'Stop! I shall tell Uncle Charles. He will hit you again!'

Edmund stopped immediately, stunned by her words.

'Leave my friends alone. You are a bully!'

'And I'll tell father you're meeting with riff raff! He won't let you out alone again. You'll have to stay in Cliff House!'

'Then I will deny it!'

'Him and his cronies beat up my brother last week,' cut in Danny, who was still on the ground.

Edmund drew breath. 'And who's your brother, then?'

Danny said nothing.

'Jack Clarke,' Edmund sneered. 'Are you a Clarke?'

Edmund began to circle Danny. Will and Perinne looked at each other, fear on their faces. Edmund's two friends had backed away. They were standing by the trees, brushing down their clothes.

'What's it to do with you?' Danny was rubbing his arm, it was hurting.

'I'll tell father you set upon me. And I'll say something is missing from the house and that your father took it. Your father will hang. Then you'll be off to the poor house!'

Will was trying to get his breath back. He stepped up behind Perinne and whispered something. She looked at him and nodded. She then went to get Pierre who had wandered off. He watched as she climbed into the saddle and rode away. Will was now bleeding from a cut on his hand and his shirt was torn. He'd had enough.

'Come, Danny, ignore 'im, let's go.'

Danny stumbled on the pebbles. 'I'm not afraid of you, Edmund Tarrant! And nor's my father,' he yelled as he and Will walked away.

The wind gusted as the pair crossed the field and away from the sea. Danny saw Will wiping blood from his hand.

'Are you all right?'

'Aye, and you?'

'Just my arm, hurts a bit. I'm sure I know one of those two with Edmund. Do you want to go to the marsh?'

'What for?'

'To look if there's anything there, maybe something that'd give us a clue.'

Will didn't reply. Then after a few minutes he stood still. 'I found somethin'.'

Danny stopped and turned. 'Found what? When?'

'That afternoon ye couldn't meet me. I found a box. Sam got loose and I saw it in the water.'

'What kind of box? Was there anything inside?'

'Not opened it yet. Couldn't open it when I tried, 'aven't

'ad time since. It's got some French writing on it.'

'So that's why you need Perinne. Trouble is she's gone now and I doubt we'll see her again.'

Will smiled. 'She's goin' to meet us again tomorrow.'

'Unless Edmund Tarrant tells his lies. We could all be in trouble.'

'Perinne didn't seem too frightened by him. She's a fiery one!'

Danny grinned. 'You're taken with her.'

'It wasn't me who blushed today!'

The boys laughed then walked on in silence until they reached Purewell from where they'd go their separate ways.

'Meet tomorrow on the beach again then?' Danny said.

'No. Meet me here,' Will replied and walked off towards the town.

## Chapter 11

# Danny in trouble again

Sir Charles Tarrant was angry. He was pacing up and down in his study at Cliff House. He'd failed to capture the shipment being brought from France and he had no idea of the whereabouts of the seven other boxes taken by the gang on the harbour. Now there'd been more trouble with Edmund. He needed to speak with James Clarke. He'd sent the new coachman for him - where was he?

Upstairs Perinne was sitting at the window of her room thinking about what to do. She'd have to be careful how she acted. Would she be brought before Sir Charles again? Who else would be there if she was - Edmund, others? And she needed to see Will and Danny, today if she could, but, if not, soon.

Yesterday afternoon she'd arrived back at Cliff House and taken Pierre to the stables. She entered the house through the door she found on her first day. She'd hoped no one would see her go in and up the back staircase to her room. Her cloak smelled, was dirty and marked with seaweed and her stockings were torn. She was in luck, but this changed later when Lucy arrived to tell her Sir Charles wanted to see her in his study and that her mother had also been sent for.

Uncle Charles looked sternly at her. 'Sit down, Perinne.'

Perinne walked over to the chair by the fireplace. The door then opened and her mother came rushing in. 'What's been happening?'

'Fighting, apparently,' Sir Charles replied.

'Fighting? Perinne, is this true?'

'I fell off Pierre.'

'Master Edmund says otherwise and that you were with two boys. Tell me the truth Perinne,' Sir Charles said.

'Boys? What boys, Perinne, who were they?' her mother sat down, shocked.

Perinne didn't like telling lies. Saying she'd fallen off her pony meant only one so far. But if she let it slip that she knew Will and Danny, let alone that she'd arranged to meet them, she'd be in trouble. She had to think quickly. She doubted her uncle would believe her about Edmund and what he'd done.

'I went for a ride on Pierre. We went down to the sea and along to see the fishing boats. Two boys were there and one of them said hello. He stroked Pierre and asked me what his name was and then Edmund appeared. He started shouting at us.'

She stopped there. That much was the truth, so far.

'Lucy says your cloak is dirty and your stockings are torn. You told her you'd fallen off your pony.'

Perinne crossed her fingers behind her back. 'Yes. He was startled. It was Edmund, he was shouting so loudly and I fell off.'

Jane put her arms around her. 'Were you hurt, darling?' She looked at her cousin. 'What has Edmund said about this?'

'According to Edmund, Perinne and the two boys attacked him and his two friends.'

Jane Menniere laughed. 'Perinne, attacked boys? Helping complete strangers! But she's a girl, and not very tall. Look at her, she's so tiny! You don't believe that, surely Charles?'

Perinne sat quietly. If the grown-ups were going to argue, she'd let them. It would mean she didn't have to say any more.

'Well, it seems that one of the boys Perinne was with is the son of one of my staff, James Clarke. I'll send for him and his boy, Daniel, in the morning. In the meantime we'll have to decide on a suitable punishment for such dreadful behaviour. Let's start with supper and breakfast in their rooms. Give them time to think about their actions!' And with that Sir Charles stormed out of the room.

'Well? Have you anything to say to me, Perinne?'

'I am sorry, maman.'

'Only sorry? You should be saying sorry to Uncle Charles. He is an important man in this town and you've brought him disgrace!'

'Edmund is a bully. He started the fight and encouraged his friends. Those boys were doing nothing wrong. I hate him!'

'You've only just met Edmund. He was helping you. Those boys could have attacked you!'

Perinne just stopped herself from saying any more. Her mother didn't know she was aware of the machine or the smugglers. Will and Danny knew something and she wanted to find out more from them. So, she'd take whatever punishment was given to her. But she would never be friends with Edmund Tarrant.

It was at first light when banging on the door startled Grandpa. He was sitting in his chair. He didn't sleep much and when he did it was usually in the parlour. He was first to the door. The tall man standing outside demanded to speak with James Clarke. Grandpa nodded and told the man to wait, he would fetch him.

When James got to the door he was shocked to find John Millar waiting for him. Millar had a smug look on his face. Since he'd arrived as new coachman two months ago he'd been trying to get into Sir Charles's favour. Always putting himself forward for extra work. And he tried to make things hard for other workers on the estate. There was something about him that James didn't like. He certainly didn't trust him.

'Yes?' said James.

'Sir Charles wants to see you now, and your son Daniel.' Millar gloated, knowing there had to be a problem.

'Bring Daniel?'

'Yes, immediately. I'll wait.'

'There's no need to wait, Millar, I know my way to Cliff House.'

Millar stood still. 'I'm to fetch you, Clarke.'

James Clarke shut the door in Millar's face with contempt.

By now Hannah was downstairs along with Jack, both woken by the noise.

'Go and fetch your brother for me, Jack, please. And have him dress in his best clothes.' James looked at Hannah. 'What's he done now?'

Danny was made to sit in the hall at Cliff House on a wooden bench beside a large door. They'd gone into the house by the back doorway. But he could now see the tall, double doors of the front entrance, which were almost as high as his cottage. Across from where he was sitting was a grand staircase with beautifully carved wooden spindles. On the walls hung paintings - one was of Sir Charles and Lady Elizabeth with a young boy, Edmund. The ceiling was decorated with garlands of plaster flowers, and from its centre, crystals of a glass chandelier hung like icicles. The candles were unlit. There was an alcove with a marble bust of a man. Danny fidgeted in the seat. His shoes were muddy from the walk and were pinching his feet. He wondered what Sir Charles would be saying to his father. He also worried about the threats Edmund had made. Maybe Perinne had told him what had really happened. Where was she? Would she be called in to see Sir Charles too? How much should he say? The questions ran through his mind again and again. It seemed an age before he heard the door open. Danny's father beckoned him inside.

Sir Charles's round face was red. He inspected Danny without speaking, his small eyes piercing. Danny tried not to look back at him. His father was standing to Sir Charles's left and slightly behind him. His face was blank, but Danny could tell he was unhappy.

'Look at me, Daniel,' Sir Charles said. His voice didn't sound as cross as Danny expected, but he was still nervous. 'I'm going to ask you some questions and I want you to tell me the truth. Do you understand?'

'Yes, sir.'

'Did you start a fight with Master Edmund?'

'No, sir.'

'What were you doing on the beach?'

'I was meeting my friend, Will.'

'And how do you know Will?'

'We met in Christchurch. I was buying fish and I

accidentally stepped on his nets.'

'His nets?'

'He mends nets and helps on a fishing boat.'

'Was he angry you stood on the net?'

'Yes, at first, but I fell and he helped me get up and picked up the fish I'd dropped.'

'When did you meet Perinne?'

'On the beach.'

Sir Charles glanced briefly round to James Clarke. 'So, who started the fight?'

'Master Edmund, sir.'

'Why do you think he started to fight you?'

Danny wanted to tell Sir Charles that his son was a bully, but he didn't want to get Perinne in trouble.

He looked at his father. 'Tell Sir Charles all you know, Daniel.'

'I don't know why. He started shouting at us, and then he pushed Will and then grabbed me.'

'And did Perinne join in?'

'Two boys were beating Will, she tried to drag them off him.'

'Edmund says you were talking to Perinne about a mystery. What is this mystery?'

Danny was horrified. He wasn't very good at thinking quickly. What could he say? Then he had an idea, which would hopefully sort Edmund out.

'Edmund attacked my brother. He said my brother was shooting on the marsh last Friday night.'

'Daniel!' James Clarke didn't want to explain the actions of another of his sons.

Sir Charles turned again to Danny's father. 'Let him carry on, James. Go on, Daniel.'

'I told Will about it. We just wondered about the shots and if it had been Master Edmund. We told Perinne. That's the mystery, whether it was Master Edmund shooting on the marsh.' Danny felt pleased with himself.

He'd given nothing away.

Sir Charles frowned. 'Master Edmund also said you were swearing oaths. Is this true?'

Danny's face reddened nearly as much as Sir Charles's.

Sir Charles continued. 'You seem to like Perinne. She needs company, but not with someone who gets her into fights and has a foul tongue.'

'But we didn't start the fight!'

'Daniel! Sir, I apologise for my son's behaviour. This boy he's got to know must be leading him into bad ways. I'll stop them from meeting.'

'No! It's not Will. Edmund is telling lies!'

Sir Charles grunted. 'Both Edmund and Perinne are being punished. They will not be allowed out of the grounds for one week. Your punishment will be for your father to administer. I think that's all for now, young man. Go and wait outside the room again.'

Danny's father flicked his head towards the door and Danny went out and back to the bench in the hall. 'What would happen now?' he thought.

'What do you think, James? Is this just children playing tom fools?'

'I don't know why he's behaving like this. He's found himself some bad company by the sounds of it. I'm sorry, sir.'

'And what of your other son? Is this true he also got himself into a scuffle with Edmund?'

James was reluctant to add to his woes, but he had no choice. 'I believe it is.'

'And this was on the marsh last Friday? Did he see anything do you think?'

'I did ask, sir, but no, not really. Just men running and he heard a cart, it may even have been our men he saw.'

'I must apologise to you, James. Edmund is a difficult boy, his mother weak with discipline and I was away far too often when he was small. I have already dealt with him. As you heard, he will be kept in as punishment, as will Perinne.'

'Thank you, Sir, I'll do the same with Daniel. And put a halt to this friendship with the town boy, Will, or whoever he is.'

'Now, let's get to our other matter?'

'I sent people into town to listen out for talk. It's all about Tom Pike's escape from gaol. That's as much as I got, no inkling of where your boxes are, Sir.'

'Hm, well, there's another problem. Jane brought with her a paper, said to be written by Monsieur Costelot himself. The boxes are all numbered, well, you've seen them. One box, the thirteenth box, contains some vital parts, without these the rest may be of little use. They must have this box, James and we don't know if they're aware of its importance.

Outside, Danny could hear his father and Sir Charles but not what they were talking about. There was no one about, so he crouched and looked through the keyhole. He could see only his father's legs. Then he heard Tom Pike's name, that some boxes were missing and one box had vital parts. Danny sat back, shocked. His father was involved with the shooting and the mystery - surely not!

## Chapter 12

# Perinne the spy

Danny was in his room changing out of his best clothes.
They were wet after the rainy walk back from Cliff House.
He was furious. He'd tried pleading with his father to give
Will a chance, telling him that it wasn't Will's fault. But his
father was angry with him. He still had to go to school, so
he'd try to see Will on his way home. Or maybe he could
ask Jack to go and see him. It was all so unfair, especially
as his father appeared to be involved. The only good thing
was that it was Wednesday and Aunt Mary came to visit
her sister and Uncle John came too. He used to play a
hand or two of cards with Grandpa, but now it was simply
talking about old times.

Perinne couldn't believe she had to stay within the grounds
of the estate. She could ride Pierre but only if one of the
footmen went with her. She hadn't spoken to Edmund but
he'd also been confined to the house. This was to be for a
whole week, and she felt she'd go mad.

The bedroom door opened and Lucy came in with a
breakfast tray.

'Mornin' Miss Perinne. Lady Elizabeth wants to know if you want to do some needlework.'

'Needlework?'

'Yes, miss. She'll be in the drawing room. It's such dull weather I expect she thinks you'll need something to occupy yourself.'

Perinne turned from the window and looked at the tray. There was milk to drink and bread, cheese and some honey. 'Where do you live, Lucy?'

'On the estate, miss. My father's John Scott. He's a footman here. He was one of the men who brought you here on the coach.'

'I can stay on the estate - maybe I can visit you?'

'I doubt that would be allowed.'

'Why not? I shall ask maman. Would you like me to visit?'

Lucy smiled. 'I'm not sure, miss. My house is very small and I have many brothers and sisters.'

'Oh, Lucy, I shall go mad stuck in the house. The estate is big enough to ride, but I cannot go alone.'

'Shall I tell Lady Elizabeth that you'll join her?'

'I suppose so.' Perinne took the tray over to the window seat and ate breakfast watching the grey and rainy day outside. Sewing. Pah!

By midday the dark clouds had been replaced by white fluffy ones and the sun was shining. Perinne asked if she could go for a walk, promising to stay close to the house. She pulled on a cloak, and laced up her boots and set out, crossing the courtyard to see Pierre. The courtyard held the stables, the dairy and some other buildings. It made a square that was the rear entrance of the house. The roofs were shiny. Steam made by the warmth of the sun was rising up from the slates and drops of water were draining onto the stony ground. The red bricks of the walls were dark with damp. At the far end an archway led out to the pathways behind Cliff House. The courtyard was also where Sir Charles's coaches were kept. Perinne wasn't sure what else the buildings were used for. Maybe this was a time to find out.

After looking in on Pierre, Perinne made her way to the next doorway. She noticed the latch was up. She peered inside and saw nothing interesting. There were ladders, boxes, small barrels she'd heard called ankers, large barrels and an assortment of tools such as hoes and scythes. Then she noticed a door at the rear. She went in and worked her way across the room. It was just a link to the next room and the door was ajar. She pulled it open slowly and peered inside. The coachman, Millar was there. He hadn't heard her. He was a tall man with broad shoulders. He wasn't wearing the wig he had on the first day she'd seen him at the Quay and his brown hair fell just above his shoulders. His face was stern looking and he had a long nose and pointed chin. She watched as he lifted the lids of boxes and barrels and slammed them down again. Unlike the stables, coach room and the one she'd just entered through, this room had a ceiling. At the far end she could now see Millar looking up at a hatch.

Suddenly he turned and moved towards Perinne who slipped quickly behind a large barrel, her heart beating rapidly. Had he heard her? Holding her breath she watched Millar take a quick look around, then, grabbing a ladder, made his way back and propped the ladder against the far wall. He stepped onto the first rung, reached to the hatch and pushed it open. Dust fell down and made him cough. He moved the ladder to the edge of the opening and climbed to the top. Soon he'd disappeared into the roof.

Perinne could hear the sound of him moving above

her, not regular footsteps but thuds. She imagined him crawling on the rafters so that he wouldn't fall through the ceiling. There was a bang and then she heard the man curse. Soon a large booted foot appeared back through the hatch feeling around for a rung. He was quickly on the ground and kicked the ladder over in temper. Perinne crouched as he came past her and went out of the door. What was he looking for? Why was he so angry? Perinne decided to follow him.

In school Danny couldn't concentrate. He'd got wet for the second time today and was in trouble for being late, despite a note from his father. He had to stay behind and catch up with the work he'd missed. Normally he'd have been angry about this, but it gave him a chance to meet Will in Purewell on the way home. After all, his father didn't know who Will was, so he could make another name up for his friend if they were seen. The time passed by slowly. The weather had got better so at least he wouldn't get wet again.

As he approached Purewell he could see Will ahead. He waved and ran towards his friend.

'Quickly,' he panted, 'over to those trees. Come on, Will, we need to hide.'

The two boys reached a small coppice. Although leaves were growing they still needed cover and moved in deeper and away from sight.

'What's 'appenin', Danny? People 'ave been asking questions. Did ye get in trouble?'

'Father's said I'm not to see you again. I have to stay in. I think Perinne must be in trouble too. She isn't allowed out of the grounds of Cliff House!'

'How do you know that?'

Danny told Will about the early morning call and being taken to Cliff House.

'We need to get to see her, Danny. So ye think Sir Charles is involved in the shooting? Is that what she wants to tell us?'

'I think so. I think Sir Charles is involved and ...,' Danny hesitated.

'Go on, and what?' Will urged.

'I think my father's involved too!'

'That must be what the shooting was about. It was the smugglers Beth heard in town against Sir Charles's men. And they were fightin' over these boxes. Maybe the box I have is part of this! What's so special about 'em, Danny? I wonder what Perinne knows. We 'ave to get a message to 'er, but how?'

Uncle John and Aunt Mary were already at the cottage when Danny arrived home. Danny threw his books onto the table and ran over to his uncle.

'Hey, Danny! I hear ye've been in a spot o' bother!'

'It wasn't me, Uncle John. Edmund Tarrant started it!'

'Edmund Tarrant? What's he to do wi' being late home last week?'

It had only been days since he had been at Hinton and walking home in the dark. He'd forgotten about being told he couldn't go to see Uncle John. Uncle John's eyes sparkled and he laughed, showing his nearly toothless mouth. He rubbed Danny's curly hair.

'Been in even more bother? There's a lad!'

Hannah Clarke came into the room with her sister. 'Don't encourage him, John. We're having no end of trouble with the boy. He's to stay in for a week except for school, no traipsing about and getting into fights!'

'Do you know any smugglers, Uncle John?'

'Danny!' Hannah Clarke shook her head. Uncle John laughed again.

'I knows 'bout pirates! 'Av I told you of the night we fought 'em to save the King's gold?'

Danny had heard it, many times, but an Uncle John story was just the thing to take his mind off the puzzles of the day. 'We were on the high seas, dark but calm, still as death. We were sailin' the *Worcester*, magnificent man-o-war, 74 guns. We'd been becalmed for two days, no sight of any ship. We were takin' gold to pay for men – mercenaries - to fight the Americans. We'd men aboard too, King's men, takin' 'em to fight. We felt safe and took to card playin' to pass the time. Then, in the middle of the night they attacked. Pirates! We 'adn't heard 'em slip up aside and sudden' they swung onto our decks. Our lookout'd been asleep. It were a mighty din. We raised the soldiers and the fightin' was savage. We lost fifteen hands that night but, we saw 'em off. Kept the gold and delivered it - and the men.'

'Now, John, filling the lad's head with your tall tales again?' It was Danny's father. 'Off to your room, Danny. Go and do some school work.'

Danny smiled at Uncle John, grabbed his books and took a lamp.

James Clarke shook his head. 'Let's go in the garden, John, we need to talk.'

Danny's bed was under the window. He put the lamp on the small table and knelt to look out at the evening. It was going dark and the sky was clear for the first time in days. The moon was rising and casting shadows. The chickens were safely in their shed softly clucking. Then he saw his father and Uncle John appear deep in conversation. Uncle John was nodding. Danny wondered what they were talking about. Why had they gone outside to talk? He turned and sat on his bed - he wasn't going to worry about grown-ups anymore. He needed to think how he could contact Perinne. If he could, then he and Will would be able to meet her on the estate.

Perinne watched as Millar made his way along the track. He was heading for a small building hidden partly by the trees. She started to follow him when suddenly someone shouted.

'Miss!' Perinne turned to see Lucy running towards her. As Lucy caught up with her, Perinne asked, 'what is that building over there Lucy?'

'Why it's the ice house, miss. Do you have ice houses in France?'

'*Oui*, er, yes, Lucy.' She'd have to follow Millar another time. But she'd take a look at the ice house tomorrow.

## Chapter 13

# The ice house

Beth was surprised to see Will at home. He usually left for work at first light. He was sitting at the table trying to open the box he'd found on the marsh. Sam was beside him gnawing greedily on a bone.

'No work today, Will?'

Will didn't look up. 'I wasn't needed on the boat today. I'm goin' later to check the nets.'

'Still trying to get into that box?'

'Hm. There don't seem to be any nails or screws. It's a strange thing.'

'Let me have a look.' Beth took the box and inspected it. 'What do these words mean?'

'I think that's a name, but I don't know 'bout the others.'

Beth noticed something along the sides. 'Look, it's just two pieces slotted together and then it's been glued. Try scraping it out.'

Will took back the box. Beth was right. It was like a simple wooden puzzle. Will patiently scraped away at the glue until a gap in the wood appeared. He could see now how easily the two pieces fitted together. He tugged and tugged and eventually the sides began to slide apart. The sides were simply a casing for another box which was appearing. Will sighed, hoping there wasn't another puzzle to solve.

'Do you think this has something to do with the boxes Adam Litty was talking about?' Beth asked him.

'Yes, and now we think Sir Charles Tarrant's involved.'

'We?'

'Me an' Danny. You met him at the Priory. Perinne knows somethin', too but we don't know what.'

'Perinne? Who's Perinne?'

She's come to live at the Tarrants'. She were at the Priory too.'

'What are you getting mixed up with Will?'

'A bit of excitement in me life for once!' Will glanced at his sister.

'You could end up in trouble!'

'Come on, Beth, it's just a bit of fun.'

Suddenly the box snapped open. The second box inside was ordinary and easily opened. Inside there was an assortment of shiny nails and tiny screws. There were two small packages each wrapped in paper and tied with string. Taking the smallest Will untied the knot then removed the paper to find an assortment of golden cogs, similar to ones found in clocks and watches. Inside the next package was a tube with thin copper wire coiled neatly around it. Will held the tube and inspected it.

'What do you think it can be?' Beth asked.

'No idea, don't look much like somethin' to shoot people o'er.' Will rewrapped the tube in its paper and placed it in the box along with the other parts. He closed the box and snapped the wooden covering back over it. 'Better keep it hidden though. Don't breathe a word about this to anyone, will ye Beth?'

'Don't worry. If it's between the town's smugglers and Sir Charles Tarrant, I want nothing to do with it. And I suggest you don't neither. Throw it in the river and have done with it.' Beth shook her head - she knew he wouldn't.

He smiled. 'Do ye know anyone workin' at Cliff House?'

Beth thought for a moment. 'Yes, Lucy Scott, she went to Mrs Tilly's school when I did. She went to Cliff House to work as a maid. Her father works there too.'

'Do ye 'ave any contact with her?'

'I sometimes see her in town. She buys cloth and silks for Lady Tarrant. Why?'

'Danny and I want to get a message to Perinne. Where does she live?'

'Out by Burton, on the edge of the estate.'

'Not far from Danny, then. Thanks, Beth.'

Beth left the room. Will rummaged around for a scrap of paper and something to write with. He carefully copied the words from the box, folded the paper and put it into his pocket.

Perinne went out straight after breakfast. She crossed the courtyard and walked along the track towards the ice house. She couldn't think what could be there other than stores and, of course, the ice. Perinne was pleased that there was an ice house. She loved cold sherbets, especially in the summer.

The ice house at Cliff House was sunken into the ground and marked by a low wall. Nearby, tall sweet-chestnut trees stood. They were offering shade now, so would be even cooler when the canopy of leaves grew from the buds that were forming. Within the wall was a short brick-built dome. Steps led down to a heavy door which was arched by bricks. The stone steps were damp and could be slippery. Perinne counted them as she carefully climbed down. There were ten. Then, at the bottom there was a step up. She imagined this was to stop rain going inside. The door was not locked. She lifted the latch and went inside, shivering at the chill of the damp air. She drew her cloak around her, and entered a passageway. The walls were entirely of brick, arched to form the ceiling. The floor was also made of brick. The only light was behind her, but she could see a tiny shaft of light ahead. She moved along towards it. The passageway split into two and she chose the one to her right from where the light appeared to be coming. There was another door. It was slightly ajar and she pulled it towards her. Inside she found herself under the dome. There was a small wall in front of her. She moved forward towards the edge of a deep pit and peered down below it. There was nothing to see but the straw that was covering the ice, so she made her way back. Just as she walked through the door, the second door on the passageway suddenly burst open. It banged against the wall. Perinne jumped, her heart beating hard in her chest. What if it were Millar?

A man came out of the door. He turned - it was the footman. He carried a plate with a joint of meat on it and he held a large ewer between his fingers.

'Hello, Miss Perinne! What are ye doing here?'

'I just wanted to see what it was like. We have an ice house in France. Is my maid, Lucy, your daughter?'

'Yes, miss.'

'She is nice. I like Lucy.'

'Lucy's a good girl, that's why she's now a lady's maid and not a maid-of-all-works. Anyhow, Miss maybe ye should go. It's cold and damp in 'ere. Don't want ye catchin' ye death, Miss.' He smiled and nodded at Perinne and soon she was back in the daylight. At least she knew there was nothing there. Maybe that's all Millar was doing yesterday, fetching something for the house, then maybe not. Whatever it was, it seemed he was looking for something. She decided she'd take a look in the roof where Millar was prying yesterday.

John Millar was sitting on a stool in a dark corner of the Eight Bells. He hadn't long. He was supposed to be on an errand in town for Sir Charles. The inn was quiet. Two old men were chattering and smoking their long, white pipes and drinking ale. They were the only others there. The landlady came in and put new logs on the fire. They spat and crackled. The door opened. In walked a bent, pale man and Millar stood up. Meekwick Ginn looked around the room with his sly, squinting eyes.

'Brandy, Landlord,' he shouted. 'Sit down,' he said to Millar. He propped his stick against the wall, removed his hat and took a seat across from him.

'Well, found anything?'

'Wherever they be, Mr Ginn, I'm sure they're not at Cliff House. I'll keep looking. No one in town has an inkling.'

Ginn made a low growl. 'My contact won't be held off for long. He wants his goods.

And what about Tarrant, is he snoopin' around for the whereabouts of ours?'

'Yes. He's had a man askin' around the alehouses, but he's got nowhere Mr Ginn.'

'I've been asked to a ball at Cliff House this coming Saturday night. I'm going. In fact, I've had an idea. Hopefully I'll do better than you useless people. I've told Pike and he's come up with a plan. This is what I want you to do.'

When Ginn had finished giving Millar his orders, he drank his brandy in one mouthful, grabbed his stick, pushed his hat back on and stormed out.

'Where've you been?' Danny was standing with his hands in his coat pockets, keeping them warm. He was glad to see Will appear in the coppice.

'Workin'. Been waitin' long?' Will answered.

'No, but I need to get back. If I'm late my family will want to know why.'

'All right, I'll be quick. I know how to get a message to Perinne. My sister Beth has a friend called Lucy Scott. She works at Cliff House and the family lives at Burton. Could ye find 'er and ask 'er to give Perinne a message?'

'Yes!' Danny's mood changed. 'I know the Scotts and her brother. Don't see her around very much, how do you know we can trust her?'

'We can't be sure, but Beth likes Lucy. I think it's our only chance. Unless we sneak into the grounds and try to see 'er.'

Danny shook his head. 'No, I don't want to do that. But I'm allowed to meet my friends. It's only you I can't see so I can go and visit her brother. I'll write a note and pass it to Lucy. If she's not there, I'll see if he'll ask her to take it.'

Perinne waited until late afternoon when the grown-ups would be settled in the drawing room. She stepped out into the courtyard. The sky was overcast and it was chilly. She made her way to the outbuilding and into the back room where she'd seen Millar go into the roof. The hatch was still open. She remembered how he'd kicked the ladder away in temper. Maybe there's nothing there and that's why he was angry, she thought. She decided she'd look in any case. The ladder was laid across the floor where it had been left. It wasn't heavy. She lifted it and stood the top against the edge of the hatch. Then she climbed until she could see inside the attic. Holes in the short walls shed light across the rafters and it smelled dusty. There were some piles of rags and some bales of straw but nothing else. She was about to start climbing back down when someone grabbed her legs. Perinne gasped and looked down to see John Millar.

'Now, what you up to little miss?' Millar snarled.

'Let go!' Perinne was stuck. She tried to kick herself free, but Millar's grasp was too strong.

'You snoopin' around? Now why's that?'

'Let go of me, I will tell Uncle Charles!'

'Don't want ye falling and hurting yourself, do we, miss?' Millar let go and Perinne climbed down the rest of the rungs. She brushed past him and quickly ran to the house.

## Chapter 14

# A door opens

Danny's main task for the day was to try to meet Lucy
Scott. His plan was to go along to see David, her brother.
That would be his excuse anyway. He'd taken a lamp up
to his room the night before. He said he was doing some
school work. This was true, but he'd also written a note for
Perinne and he hoped Lucy would agree to take it to her.
But that was before his father called him downstairs. Jack
was already there. 'What now?' thought Danny.

'Now sons,' James Clarke began. 'I've been most
displeased lately with your fights and such. But, Sir Charles
seems less bothered. He's asked me to take you along to
Cliff House this Saturday. There's to be a grand ball and
you're both needed to help out.'

Danny couldn't believe his luck. He'd be able to speak
with Perinne!

'Guests will be coming from all over Hampshire and
Dorset. There'll be lords and ladies and the Duchess of
Dorset with Lady Mary. There aren't enough staff at Cliff
House to cope, so Sir Charles is asking in the town for
people to help out. I said you'll both help as forfeit for your
recent bad behaviour. But Sir Charles is going to pay you!'
James Clarke smiled at his two sons. 'You'll be needed
all day and he'll pay you sixpence each if you perform
your duties well. Jack, you'll join the footmen. You'll be

helping with the horses and receiving the carriages. Danny you're to help with serving.'

'Serving? I don't know how to do that!'

'I'm sure you'll both pick up your duties easily. You're to be given special clothes to wear. But most of all I want you to keep as far away from Edmund as possible. Is that understood?'

'Yes, father,' the boys said in unison.

'And if he teases you then you take no notice. I hope you both take heed.'

Danny tried not to let anyone see his excitement. Things had changed, and he'd had an idea. It wasn't Perinne he needed to get a message to now, it was Will.

School on a Friday was no different from any other day. But today they were learning science and geography. The boys were told about some new inventions. There were engines that ran on steam, and a machine that could spin eight threads at the same time. Danny was intrigued to hear about a suit that allowed men to walk under water. He loved this. He also enjoyed his geography lessons, especially hearing about voyages to fantastic places around the world. He was fascinated by stories about the wondrous things that could be seen and the exotic animals that lived in far-away places. The day passed by quickly. After school he ran down to the quayside. He soon spotted Master Hardyman's boat but couldn't see Will. He walked from the quayside towards the High Street, passing the Poor House. He could hear a child crying and there was shouting. Other children were running around in the street, some without shoes. He arrived in Church Street. He remembered that Will had said his sister Beth worked at the George, so he crossed over the road and went inside. He saw her. She was as pretty as he remembered her. She was smiling and carrying a tray of tankards. Her skirts, covered by a white linen apron, swirled as she walked and she wore a white blouse and over this a brown bodice. Her dark hair was tied up and hidden under a lace bonnet.

'Hello, young Sir, and how can we be of service to you this afternoon?'

Danny turned to see a jolly-faced woman. She was short and plump and she was wearing an apron like Beth's and a mob cap.

'I'm looking for my friend.'

'And 'ere I am!' The familiar voice of Will sounded from behind him. Danny turned. 'It's all right, Mistress Martin, he's lookin' for me.'

Will took Danny by the arm and led him down the road, passing the old thatched house on the way towards the ancient castle.

'What's goin' on? I thought ye were goin' to see Lucy this afternoon? What if we're seen together?'

The boys climbed over the stones and scrambled up the hill to the castle ruins. They sat down between the arch of a doorway in one of the thick walls, hidden from sight.

'I'm going to Cliff House!' Danny started.

'When?'

'On Saturday. And you could be there too!'

'Me? An' 'ow's that?'

'Father says they've been asking around town for help. You could volunteer. People have to go to the gates in the morning.'

'Danny, aren't ye forgettin' somethin'?'

'What? It's a great chance Will!'

Will plucked at the grass. 'Three days ago, Danny, we were fightin' with Edmund Tarrant. I doubt I'd be let in! And if I did get in, what'd happen when *he* saw me?'

'I'd forgotten.' Danny paused. 'I *know*. We can *disguise*

you! You can put your hair up in a bonnet and wear some of Beth's clothes. You look just like each other!'

'No, Danny. *NO*.'

'Yes! It's perfect.'

'Are you forgettin' somethin' else? I've no idea what girl's work is in a big house. It's a stupid idea, Danny. I'd be caught straight away. In any case, I'm *not* dressin' up as a girl. *Never*!' Danny began to laugh, then Will started laughing too and before long the boys were laughing until their sides ached.

The sun was going down. Clouds in the west were glowing red. 'I've got to get back home. Think about it, Will. It's a week since this whole thing started and we're no nearer to knowing what's going on. We need to get together with Perinne. Turn up at the gates tomorrow morning. They may just choose you.'

'Oh, miss, it's going to be so grand!' Lucy was hanging Perinne's cloak in the wardrobe and looking through the dresses hanging there. Perinne was sitting staring out of the window. 'Do you know what you'll be wearin', miss?'

'I believe maman has bought something new for me. What is this grand ball for, Lucy?'

'It's for her Ladyship's birthday.'

'But she seems not to care too much for people?'

'You mustn't say that, miss. The mistress is just a quiet sort, that's all. The house is going to be full. We've had to air all the rooms and put out all the best linen and the best china and silver's coming out too.'

'I saw your father yesterday, at the ice house.'

'He'd be checking the meats for the weekend. There's going to be venison and beef and duck and pigeon. And he'd be checkin' the ice.'

'I like your father but I do not like Millar. He does not seem honest. Your father does, though.'

'Why do you say that about Mr Millar, miss?'

'He does not seem to do anything. Your father is busy, but Millar seems only to be walking around all the time.'

'Well he's sure to be busy tomorrow, everyone will be. They're even bringin' people up from the town to help out. Even Mr Clarke's boys are coming.'

Perinne sat up. Danny's going to be here, but what about Will?

James Clarke had to look twice. Was that Danny? Who was he with? Is *he* the boy Will? He watched as the two boys scuttled across the road and down the street towards the castle. What were they up to? But he wasn't too concerned about Will now, not since he'd spoken with Hardyman. At the moment he needed to get to the post and excise office to check if he'd had a reply to his letter. If none had arrived, the next post was Saturday morning and he'd be at Cliff House all day.

Isaac Hooper walked past James Clarke and onto the High Street. He had things on his mind. He knew there was something Adam Litty wasn't telling him about and he knew it had something to do with Tom Pike. Most of the town now knew he'd escaped from gaol. He was about too, people had seen him, though rumour was he was in hiding again in the Forest. Isaac also knew Meekwick Ginn had a hand in whatever was going on. That could mean only one thing - there was money in it for those involved. Just as he passed the window of the Misses Pilgrim's millinery and drapery shop, Beth Gibbs came out.

'Beth!'

'Hello, Isaac.' Beth lifted her skirts from the ground and kept walking, stepping up her pace. It was obvious that Isaac had been on the ale again.

'How's things at the George? Many strangers about?'

'Ye should ask Mistress Martin 'bout that, Isaac.'

'How 'bout Tom Pike?'

'I don't know Tom Pike.'

'Ye know Adam Litty though.'

'Mr Litty's often in.'

'Maybe ye've seen a strange-lookin' man - bent, pale face.'

Beth ignored him.

'Come on, Beth, he's an old friend an' I 'eard he were in town.'

Beth doubted that, Isaac was fishing for information. 'Sorry, Isaac, ye need to ask the Landlord of goings on, not me.' She raced on ahead without looking back.

Isaac stopped. He was swaying. 'How's ye mother?' He shouted after her.

He slumped down on a low wall near the town pound, where stray animals were held. There were none there, it was too late in the day. Beth's face had changed when he'd described Ginn. He'd been there all right, so had Pike and Litty. They'd have used Forest tracks to bring Pike back to avoid the turnpikes. The strange thing was he knew something had been smuggled in last week and there'd been a fight over it. Litty and Ginn had asked him the next day if he knew if anything unusual had come in. But nothing different had been around for sale. Isaac lifted his hat and scratched his head. There was someone he knew who'd dealt with strange cargoes before - John Hewitt. But that meant a trip to Hinton. Isaac decided that if he didn't get work at Cliff House tomorrow, he'd go to Hinton instead.

## Chapter 15

# A secret revealed

Danny, Jack and James Clarke walked to Cliff House early on Saturday morning. News of a day's work had spread and several people were already gathered at the gates. Danny looked to see if Will was with them, but he couldn't spot him. Then he chuckled to himself. Perhaps he was in disguise! They walked up the stony path towards the rear of the house and entered the courtyard. James Clarke looked around. He saw Millar first of all and groaned.

'These your lads, Clarke?' Millar sneered.

Jack looked at his father. He remembered how Millar had woken them all a few mornings before, hammering on the door.

Millar looked Jack up and down. 'Bit of a skinny one.'

James Clarke ignored the remark and was relieved when Millar shouted out, 'Scott! Out here! Here's yer help.' Then he walked off.

'Did you see his feet?' Danny laughed. 'They were huge!'

'He can't help that, Danny. Don't make fun of Millar.'

John Scott came out of the stables. He was a short, slim man. His greying hair was cut short under his cap and he walked with a slight limp. 'Hello, Mr Clarke,' he said smiling at the boys. 'Who do we 'ave 'ere then?'

'This is Jack, he's here to help you,' James said relieved.

'Danny here is working in the house.'

'Come on then, Jack, let's get on with it. Thank ye, Mr Clarke.'

Soon Danny and his father were in a large room. Inside was the longest table Danny had ever seen. Alongside this was a bench and at one end four young girls, each wearing maids dresses, aprons and caps were sitting eating. Danny looked at them, if only I could remember what Lucy looked like, he thought. They passed through the door at the far end of the room and into a kitchen.

'Good morning, Susan,' James Clarke smiled at a plump woman with a jolly face and sparkling eyes who was standing at a table kneading a large lump of dough.

'Ah! Mr Clarke, expect this is young Daniel then?'

'Yes, here he is, and all ready to be set to work.'

Susan stopped kneading and wiped her brow with the back of her hand, leaving a floury streak. 'Ye can leave 'im with me, Mr Clarke, Joseph'll be here soon an' we can set 'im at his tasks.'

'Thanks, Susan. I'm here all day and if he's any trouble, send for me.'

Danny frowned and Susan winked at him as she went back to kneading the dough. The room had a high ceiling and hanging from it were two candle holders. They were unlit as plenty of light passed through the window. Behind Susan was a huge fireplace with iron stands. Metal pans, set on a cast-iron hob, were hissing with steam and the lids rattled. To one side were iron rails where large spoons, knives and ladles were hanging. On the other side, shelves groaned with shiny pots and glinting pans of all sizes. Another wall was hidden by a large dresser with row upon row of plates and dishes. A loud clattering sound was now coming from the other room. Danny stretched to see what the noise was. Susan chatted away about the guests arriving and all the breads, meats and pies she had to prepare for the weekend.

'I hope the extra kitchen maid arrives soon, I need help with all this, or it won't be ready in time,' she said.

'Could I not help?' Danny enquired.

'Don't you go stealin' my help, Susan!' A hand fell on Danny's shoulder. Behind him a stocky man wearing a short wig and black coat, pants and white stockings appeared. 'Come on, Daniel, or is it Danny? Let's get you started on your tasks.'

'It's Danny, sir.'

'Call me Joseph, everyone else does.'

They returned to the room with the long table. The girls were now standing at the doorway receiving instructions from an older woman. On the table a large, rough cloth had been laid. Two basins were set at the edge and next to this a pile of small cloths. Danny looked on amazed. The table was covered in an array of silver salvers, plates, dishes and pots of all shapes and sizes. Almost from one end to the other, silver knives, forks, spoons and serving ladles were lying side by side. In the centre were four large candleholders.

'Here you are, Danny, set yourself down. I'll get you an apron and you can start cleaning these.'

Danny's jaw dropped as he scanned the sight. Oh *no*!

Perinne was pleased that none of the footmen would have time to go with her on her ride today. She was also pleased Edmund hadn't been asked to go with her in their place. She might even get a chance to talk to Danny today. The sun was shining and she was looking forward to seeing all the grand people arriving for the ball. This would be a good day. She walked over to the stables and found her pony already saddled. There was a boy with Scott, she thought he looked like Danny. Jack smiled at Perinne. Danny had asked him to look out for her.

John Scott spoke first. 'This is Jack, miss. He's helpin' today. He's one of Mr Clarke's boys.'

'Hello, Jack,' Perinne smiled. Jack nodded.

Scott took Pierre's reins and led the pony into the courtyard. Jack took his chance. 'Danny asked me to say he'll try to speak with you,' he whispered. 'He's helping with serving, so he'll be in the house most of the day I expect.'

'Oh?' Perinne hesitated. 'Thank you, Jack.' Did he know about the mysterious machine and the missing boxes, she wondered. He hadn't mentioned Will. Lucy had said men folk from the town were helping with the grounds so maybe Will was helping too. The recent wet and windy weather had left it untidy and unkempt. Sir Charles had said he wanted to make a good impression tonight, though she didn't know why. She'd look out for Will on her ride and try to speak with Danny later.

As Will approached the gates at Cliff House he spotted old Isaac ahead of him. A man holding a wooden staff was talking to people who either went in through the gates to stand with others gathered inside or were turned away. Isaac was easy to spot as he approached the man who shook his head. Isaac lifted his arms as though pleading but didn't persist and walked away. Will thought about hiding. He didn't want to speak to him, but Isaac headed away towards the Forest. When it was Will's turn the man smiled.

'Can you use a scythe, lad?'

'Aye,' Will replied. Well, he'd only had a go once but

wasn't going to admit to it.

'Over there please. Next!'

Will walked over to the group. He recognised one or two men from the town. They nodded to each other, then stood and waited. It wasn't long before the man had dismissed the rest of the crowd and closed the gates. He introduced himself as head gardener and said they were to help tidy the grounds. He also asked if anyone was available to help with coaches later to let him know. Will hoped Edmund wouldn't be around to notice him, but how would he let Danny know he was here. Soon Will and three other men were given orders to spread out. They had to cut the long grass beside the driveway leading to the front of the house. After this, they would go on to clear the grass at the rear. Others were clipping at shrubs and bushes. A fire was lit and white drifts of smoke rose, swirling in the breeze that had picked up over the past hour. Will liked the woody smell. The men with whom he was working with seemed cheerful, singing as they swung their scythes. Even if nothing happens at least I'll earn a shilling, thought Will.

It was Perinne who saw Will first, his familiar pony tail visible against the back of his shirt. His sleeves were rolled up and he was swinging a scythe, shearing through the long grass. She nudged Pierre with her heels and trotted towards him.

'Hello, Will.'

Will stopped cutting.

'Hello, Perinne, be careful talkin' to me 'ere, someone may see us. The man at the gate asked for extra 'elp, so I'm stayin' all day. I'll be up at the house after dark. We're bein' given supper, so I'll try to get together wi' Danny then. Will you tell us what's goin' on?' He looked around. Only the three men were visible.

'I will tell you now.' Perinne told Will what she'd overheard.

He laughed and shook his head. 'No, that can't be! Ye don't believe that do ye? A machine that lets people talk to each other, from town to town? Come on, Perinne, that's impossible! Do ye believe it?'

Perinne sniffed and rubbed her nose. 'Why would Uncle Charles talk about it that way if it were not so and why are people fighting over it?'

'That's true enough. So where is it?'

'Uncle Charles has six boxes and there are thirteen altogether, but he does not know where the others are. I do not think they are here at Cliff House. The coachman, Millar, has been snooping. I think that is what he was looking for ... Atishoo! It is the grass, Will, these things and flowers, they make me sneeze.'

'So, if we can find out who 'as the other boxes, or where they're 'idden, there might be a reward?'

'I do not know. Tssss ... I will try to find out.'

Will gave a sudden gasp. 'Go Perinne, someone's comin. We'll try to meet up later.'

As Perinne rode off another rider was coming towards Will. It was Edmund Tarrant! Will tucked his hair into his cap and pulled it as low over his face as it would go. He grabbed the scythe and began slicing it through the long grass. The hooves drummed louder and louder. Will held his breath.

'Perinne, wait!' Edmund's voice growled. Will didn't look up and moved to keep his back to the fast-approaching horse.

'Perinne!'

Edmund's horse thundered past.

Will took off his cap and wiped his brow. Phew! That

was a close call. He thought about what Perinne had told him - I wonder if the box I have is one of the missing ones... .

## Chapter 16

# The grand ball

Perinne was sitting on the seat by the window in her room. She hadn't enjoyed much of a ride before Edmund had been sent to bring her back to the house as her bath was ready, but she hadn't minded. She hadn't bathed since her arrival the week before and the warm water had been lovely.

The door opened and Lucy came in holding a dress over her arm and carrying a basket.

'What have you there, Lucy?'

'Some ribbons and beads for your hair, miss.' Lucy laid the dress and basket on the bed and walked over to the window.

'No one has arrived yet, it seems very soon to get ready. Will we be able to watch the coaches arrive?'

'I think the mistress will want you downstairs, miss.'

'And do we wear masks? We wear masks at balls in France.'

'Yes, and lovely gowns for the ladies and gentlemen in all their finery. And the Duchess of Dorset and Lady Mary are coming. They're to be overnight guests. It's going to be so beautiful, miss.'

Perinne jumped up, crossed her arms and grabbed Lucy by the hands, spinning her around.

'Yes, I *love* the contredanse!'

The two girls spun until they were dizzy and fell onto the bed laughing. 'Oh, miss, that was fun but I shouldn't. I'll be in such trouble.'

'Nonsense, Lucy. Will you be at the ball?'

'Yes, miss, helping to serve drinks and there'll be some supper to serve too.'

'Have you seen Danny?'

'Danny?'

'Mr Clarke's son. You said he was helping also.'

Lucy laughed. 'Yes, he's here and he's been busy polishing the silver. Not too happy about it either by the look on his face. He'll be helping me later. How do you know him, Miss?'

Perinne didn't answer. 'Come on Lucy, help me to get ready!'

Joseph kept Danny busy all day. He took him to the dining room where supper and drinks would be set out and asked him to fold napkins into a neat pile. 'Lucy will tell you your duties from now on.' Joseph smiled and left the room.

Danny watched a footman place dozens of candles wherever he could find a space. This was despite there being oil lamps. Furniture was being brought through from the drawing room to make space for the dancing later on. Danny had almost completed his task when one of the girls he'd seen at breakfast came in.

'Hello, Danny. I'm Lucy. You'll be helping me tonight, then?'

Danny smiled. 'Are you Perinne's maid?'

'And what if I am?' Lucy replied.

'I need to speak with her.'

'Now why would Miss Perinne want to speak with a

servant boy?' She teased.

'I'm *not* a servant!' Danny checked himself. He didn't want to make an enemy of Lucy. 'Sorry, I didn't mean to shout. I'm just helping out. I go to school, I don't work.'

'Well, *you're* a lucky one,' she smiled. 'I should think that Miss Perinne will be far too busy dancing with the young gentlemen guests to bother with you. Come on, I'll show you what to do.'

'You! Hey there, boy, come 'ere!' Will turned as a man approached him. 'Are you the lad that volunteered to help at the stables?'

'I am that.'

'Well, come with me. I'm Millar,' he mumbled over his shoulder as he hurried away.

Will followed the man towards the stables. He thought that it had to be the same man who Perinne had caught poking around. Maybe he could find out more about him. Being near the house might also give him a chance to talk to Danny and tell him what Perinne had said. He'd have to risk being seen by Edmund.

Coach after coach drove up the long drive to the front of Cliff House. The sun was going down and light was catching on the metal of the harnesses, flashing as though fireflies were circling around them. If the coaches had their own footmen the house servants would stay by the entrance. Some people drove themselves and they would be helped down and the coach driven around to the courtyard to be looked after. If the guests were staying for the weekend, the horses were unharnessed and rested in the stables.

Perinne was in the hall. She wore her new dress which was pale pink. Spring flowers had been put into vases and placed on shelves and a nearby table. She could already feel her nose tickling. Uncle Charles and Lady Elizabeth were greeting the guests and then introducing them to her maman and Perinne herself. Footmen dressed in fine green waistcoats, brown breeches and white stockings took coats and hats away. Perinne wished she didn't have to be there. Her maman seemed flustered and kept looking at the door. Perinne watched too as the next coach arrived and was puzzled to see it was Uncle Charles's. The coach drew up and John Scott, now dressed in full livery, jumped down, opened the coach door and pulled down the steps. A man stepped out. He was tall and handsome.

'Papa!'

There were two doors in the same wall, one opening into the kitchen and the other into the dining room. 'To stop the smells goin' through,' Lucy had told Danny. Danny's job wasn't serving food but making sure that the servants could get through the doors without trouble. He now wore a smart, green waistcoat and shirt like the other men servants. He watched as Joseph welcomed the guests. Two servant girls were holding drinks on silver trays Danny had polished earlier. After the guests collected a drink, another servant led them towards the large drawing room. The men and women were dressed in the finest clothes Danny had ever seen. The women were in long wide-waisted dresses of whites, purples and reds; all the men wore wigs. They wore lace cravats and white shirts and over velvet breeches were long-tailed coats. They were all wearing masks. Then a girl came in, Danny thought it had to be Perinne. The girl's hair was tied up in ribbons, but it was dark like Perinne's. She was holding a man's hand and a woman followed behind, smiling - it must be her mother, thought Danny, but who was the man? The three walked past and the girl turned towards Danny and nodded - it had to be Perinne.

Sounds of stringed instruments mixed with chattering voices were coming from the drawing room. More guests passed by, some families with parents and their sons and daughters. Next a man came in alone. He was bent and walked with a stick. He was wearing a short, grey wig and a black mask which made his pale skin almost shine. Then a woman with a girl, both in the most elaborate gowns, passed by.

'That's the Duchess,' one of the servant girls whispered to the other, then curtsied as the women passed by. Finally, Sir Charles and Lady Tarrant with Edmund came in. They were wearing masks, but Danny knew it was them.

The evening began and Danny watched as couples danced minuets. As the night wore on the music changed. The revellers grouped and wove the most elaborate and lively dances. Sometimes Danny was asked to fetch drinks from the kitchens. Joseph also asked him to collect up used glasses and goblets. His tray was nearly full when he spotted a glass standing in an alcove next to a vase. Avoiding the dancers, he moved carefully down the room and, putting the tray onto a chair, he reached for the glass. But one of the servants, who'd arrived with the guests, brushed by and knocked his back. He fell forward and struck the vase. It started to topple and Danny reached out to catch it. He grabbed it just in time, but twisted and fell, knocking the tray of glasses onto the floor and smashing them. A dancer, a girl, stopped and gasped. Danny landed with a bump on the floor with the vase intact. The music came to a halt and everyone in the room turned and looked at Danny.

Joseph and Lucy dashed across the room and helped him to his feet. Another figure approached.

'You!' Edmund sneered, then turned and walked away towards another boy.

Joseph took the vase and placed it back in the alcove. Another servant was sent for a brush.

'I'm sorry, Joseph, I couldn't help it.' Danny wondered how much trouble he'd be in now. Would his father be called in?

But Joseph smiled. 'Come on, Danny, it was an accident, help Lucy clear this up, quickly now!'

The musicians started to play and the guests began chatting. The pair soon had everything cleared and the dancing began again. 'Go and get some fresh air,' Joseph said, patting Danny on his back.

Danny went out towards the courtyard. Lamps had been set up and with these and the light from the kitchen he could see the stables. He'd go and see how Jack was getting on. Coaches and horses were standing over to one side. Danny wondered if it would be Jack looking after them.

'Wait, Danny!'

Danny turned. It was Perinne.

'I told maman I needed the necessary!'

'And do you?' Danny laughed. 'I'm going to see if Jack's all right and I wonder if Will managed to get in.'

'Yes, he did, I have seen him today,' Perinne replied.

As the two walked across the courtyard in the pale light of the oil lanterns, they didn't notice a figure watching them.

'Danny, Perinne!' a hushed voice sounded so quietly the pair didn't hear it at first. 'Danny!'

Danny turned and looked across to the coaches. It was Will! Danny and Perinne glanced around to see if anyone could see them, then ran over to him. 'Come on!' Will said, opening the door of one of the coaches. Danny and Perinne climbed inside and Will followed them. The horses whinnied. 'They'll be fine,' he said.

The coach had two wide seats. Will sat down across from Danny and Perinne. 'Tell Danny 'bout the machine, Perinne. See if he believes ye.'

Perinne repeated what she'd said to Will that morning.

'See, nonsense. Don't ye think so Danny?'

Danny shifted in his seat. 'There are many new inventions. We learn about them at school. But this one does sound impossible.'

'It is only what I heard.'

'So, what do we know?' Danny started. 'There were shots on the marsh. There are boxes missing.'

'Uncle Charles has six and there are thirteen altogether and number thirteen is the most important.'

'And some o' the town's smugglers know 'bout the others,' Will chipped in. 'Tom Pike has somethin' to do with it.'

'But it wasn't him on the marsh,' Danny replied. 'I think the smugglers I saw in the Forest were on their way to get him.'

'And there was the pale man with a stoop who Beth saw with Tom Pike and Adam Litty. I saw him with old Isaac as well,' said Will.

'Old Isaac?' Perinne asked.

'Pale man? Stooped?' Danny gasped. 'There's a man like that here tonight. Perinne, you must have noticed him?'

'I confess not. My papa has arrived from France. It was a big surprise. I have been so happy tonight I have not noticed.'

'What are we goin' to do?' Will asked.

'We could find out where the smugglers have the other boxes and tell Sir Charles. We may get a reward!' Danny beamed.

'I am not sure that they belong to Uncle Charles,' Perinne cut in.

'Then we 'ave to find out *who* they belong to and try to get all the boxes back to 'em, or at least let 'em know where they are,' Will said, 'but 'ow?' Then Will remembered something. He pulled a piece of paper from his breeches pocket and showed it to Perinne. 'I found a box in the water by the marsh. This was written on it. What does this say?'

Perinne held the paper towards the window hoping the light from one of the lamps would help. '*M Costelot* - it is a name. *Privé* is private and *Treize* is thirteen. Costelot, that is the name of the inventor! That is what I heard Uncle Charles say. The boxes hold parts of the machine. You have the thirteenth box!

Suddenly the coach jolted and began to move. Perrine grabbed hold of Danny to stop herself falling onto the floor.

'Garrgh ...!' A masked face appeared at the window. Perinne screamed. The man opened the door. Long hair straggled down from underneath a round felt hat and he was wearing a servant's green waistcoat. Will tried to stand and push the man away, but the man brushed by him and climbed onto the seat. Will then lunged to pull him up, but the movement of the coach made him unsteady. Danny began punching the man.

'Cod's head!' Perinne joined in, remembering how Danny had insulted Edmund. She began kicking at the man's shins.

'Ye little varmints!' The man grabbed Will. 'Stop kickin' or out he goes!'

The coach rocked and the rattle of the gravel track and horses' hooves roared in their ears.

'Get him!' Will shouted.

The man drew a pistol and first pointed it at Danny

and Perinne then pushed Will towards the door which was swinging open. Will tried to grab the pistol but lost his balance, grasping hold of the sides of the coach. With his free hand the man thumped at Will's hands and Will tumbled out into the darkness.

He rolled. Luckily he'd fallen onto grass. He jumped up as the coach rumbled away. It was no good chasing it, he'd never catch it. He needed to get back to the house and raise the alarm.

## Chapter 17

# Kidnapped!

'Was that someone screaming?' Jack asked John Scott. They were eating bread and some meat pieces that Susan had sent over to the stables.

'Some of the young guests makin' mischief I expect,' John replied biting into another chunk.

Suddenly there was a sound of wheels and hooves crunching in the courtyard.

'What's that? Come on Jack!' They got outside in time to see one of the coaches disappearing through the courtyard entrance and into the grounds. 'That's odd. Wasn't expectin' anyone to be leaving yet.'

A shout came from the doorway of the house. 'Scott! Have you seen Miss Perinne?' It was Sir Charles.

'No, sir, but a coach just left.'

'A coach?'

'Just 'eard it, sir. It were too late to see who it was.'

'What's that?' Edmund appeared. 'Over there.' He pointed to a dark silhouette running towards the house. Then he saw Jack. 'Why's he here, father?'

'Never mind that, who's this coming towards us?' Sir Charles stepped forward.

'It's that ruffian from the town. What's he doing here? I'll see him off!' Edmund ran towards the figure.

'Wait! Edmund, come back!'

By now Perinne's mother and father had appeared along with James Clarke and some of the guests and servants. The crowd watched as Edmund ran off. The approaching person stopped and Edmund's voice could be heard shouting.

'Edmund!' Sir Charles set out after his son, followed by James Clarke and Yves Menniere, Perrine's father.

Will could see Edmund approaching followed by three men.

'What do you want, lout? Get off our land!'

'I need to see yer father!'

'Go away!'

'Step back, Edmund!' the voice of Sir Charles boomed behind him. 'What is it, lad?'

Will's hands fell to his knees, his tall frame bending. He was panting.

'Perinne, sir, an' - Danny. We – were – talkin', a man – he's got Perinne an' Danny.'

'Danny?' James Clarke stepped forward. 'What were you all doing? What man?'

They led Will back towards the house.

'Take him to the kitchen, James, see what you can get out of him. Scott! Saddle up some horses! Where's Millar, we need him? Come on! They can't have got far!'

Danny stared at the man. Would he shoot them? He noticed a second pistol in the man's belt. The coach ground to a halt and someone jumped down.

'Hurry!' A voice growled from above. Three of them thought Danny and that voice? There was something familiar about it. It was the same as the one in the Forest. They're the men from the Forest! 'Get rid of the boy!' the voice bellowed.

The first man was still pointing the pistol at Danny and Perinne. The coach door opened. Another man, his face also masked and wearing a dark hat with a wide brim pulled low over his brow, reached out and grabbed Danny, pulling him from the coach.

'Get off him, you brute!' Perinne shouted.

'Shut up!' the man waved the pistol in her face. 'I aint afraid to use this!'

'Do as he says, Perinne.' Danny kicked and wriggled as much as he could, but the man was as strong as an ox. He lifted Danny, crushing his arms by his sides, and held him in one arm as if he were a bundle of straw. His rough coat rubbed against Danny's face. The man slammed the door closed and the coach sped off again. Danny kicked out and twisted. The man was too strong for him. He even tried to bite, but the man's sleeve was too thick.

'Keep still!'

Danny knew this voice too. Who was it? The man strode across the darkness back towards the house. What's going on? Danny didn't understand. For a moment he wondered if he were being rescued. He could see the entrance to the courtyard. Flames from torches showed people running around and Danny could hear shouting. But the man rushed past, keeping as near to the trees and bushes as possible.

'Where are you taking me? Let me go!' Danny shouted.

'Shut ye bone box!'

The man clamped his hand across Danny's mouth as more shouting echoed out into the night. Figures now appeared to be running out of the courtyard exit and towards them. The man quickly moved into the shrubbery and waited. Danny could hardly breathe as the man kept his vice-like grip around him and his clammy palm on his face. After several minutes the people returned towards the house and the man started to move again. Danny could just make out horses which were being held as people mounted them, then despaired as he saw them set off from the house along the driveway and away from him. Even if he were able to scream for help, they were too far in the distance to have any chance to hear him. Soon the man was taking him down some steps. He looked at the ground as the man stepped cautiously. It was difficult to see, but he appeared to have long feet, just like Millar. The man took his hand from Danny's mouth and opened a door. Where was he? Oh, *no*! thought Danny, an ice house!

'Get in there!' He threw Danny to the floor. It was hard and damp. The door slammed and Danny heard a bolt slide across. It was freezing cold. He was only wearing a servant's waistcoat and shirt. He was in the ice house and couldn't get out. He banged on the door.

'Help! Help! Let me out!'

But no one came. Danny slumped to the floor. 'What should I do?' he thought. The air was dank and bitter, and he didn't know where the ice was. 'If I fall onto that I'll freeze to death! But I can't give in.'

Will was now in the servant's room. He was sitting at the long table and Susan had given him a drink of ale. James Clarke was standing next to him.

'I'm Danny's father. Are you sure you didn't recognise the man, Will?' he asked.

'No, sorry Mr Clarke, they 'ad masks and it were dark.'

The door banged open. 'What's going on?' Millar strode in and threw his hat onto the table.

'Where've you been?' James demanded.

'Nothin' to do with you!'

'Yes it is! You're responsible for the stables and coaches.

One's just been stolen and they've taken Miss Perinne and my son at pistol point!'

'I was on an errand for Sir Charles. Mind your own business, Clarke!'

Millar turned to Will. 'What did ye see? Did ye know these men?'

'Leave him, Millar, he doesn't know anything. But I want to know whose coach is missing.'

Millar snarled, grabbed his hat and stormed back outside.

Word about Perinne had reached the revellers. The dancing had stopped. The ladies had gathered around a tearful Jane Menniere and Lady Elizabeth. Joseph organised the servants to fetch the cloaks and hats for the guests who were going home and rouse their footmen and coach drivers to bring the coaches to the front of the house. Lucy was asked to see to the guests staying overnight and take them to their rooms. But she was in tears also, finding it hard to think about her duties.

'Oh, Joseph, what's happened? Who's taken Miss Perinne?'

'Don't worry, Lucy. The master'll find 'em and he'll bring the full weight of the law down on 'em . They'll hang for this!'

'Shall I see if Her Grace and Lady Mary are ready to retire?'

'No, leave them with the mistress and Madame Menniere for now. Get 'em some brandy.'

Will lifted his head from his hands. 'I want to 'elp find Perinne and Danny.'

'People are out there looking for them now, lad,' James Clarke's face was furrowed with worry. 'I want to look too, but I need to wait here until I'm needed. Look, go home and come to our house in the morning. Hopefully they'll be found by then but if not, you can help me then. I'll see if there's a coach going your way and you can take a lift.'

'No, I think I'll walk.'

'But it's nearly an hour's walk into town, it's gone ten o'clock and dark as pitch. And you've had a shock.'

'Thanks Mr Clarke, I'll walk. I need to think.'

'If you're sure. I'll get a lamp for you. You can return it tomorrow.'

Will was given an old coach lamp, which gave off a waxy odour. He set out from the house. He didn't want to go home, not with Perinne and Danny out there with those men. Where could they be? He walked out of the courtyard and peered out into the darkness. Above the trees the night was clear. Stars glittered across the black, moonless sky. Then he heard a noise. At first he thought it was an owl. But there was another noise with it, a drumming noise. He lifted the lamp and looked around. The light was weak and didn't cast very far but it was enough to catch the sight of eyes peering directly towards him. It made him gasp at first, then he realised it was a small herd of deer. Thump, thump, thump, *ell*, *ell*. That sounds like 'help' thought Will. He stood still and strained to hear the noise again. It was coming from just beyond the house. He moved carefully towards the sounds. The deer, startled, ran off into the trees. Thump, thump, thump ... '*Help, help*!' Will quickened his pace. He could see a mound ahead with a low brick wall. '*Help! Help*!' The cry was clear now. Will made his way down a set of steps and with the light from the lamp he could see a door. It was bolted. He pulled the bolt across and lifted the latch. 'Danny?'

'Will! How did you find me? I'm lucky you did.'

Will helped Danny up the steps. 'Let's get ye back to the house. Ye're freezin'! Ye father's worried out of his mind,' Will said.

'What about Perinne?'

They've gone lookin' for 'er.'

'It was the smugglers, Will. The driver, it was the same voice as last Friday night in the Forest, the night they freed Tom Pike from gaol. It must be the smugglers who've got her!'

'Why though?'

'I don't know. But we have to find her, Will. And I know who else is involved!'

Perinne's heart was thumping in her chest, but she was determined not to let the man see how frightened she was. He was thin, his face below the mask was whiskery and the man's teeth were bad. He smelled terrible.

'Stop ye starin' at me.' He put the pistol back into his belt. 'I aint goin' to hurt ye. Just doin' what's asked o' me, that's all.'

Perinne stayed quiet. The darkness meant she couldn't see where she was. Even if she could, she doubted she'd know where they were. Everything was unfamiliar. The coach slowed and came to a stop. It rocked as the driver got off. The door opened.

'Out you get, young miss, come on.'

'*Non*!'

The man reached for his pistol again. Perinne scowled and got up. The driver held out a hand to help her down.

'Do not touch me!'

'Bring that blanket, ye'll need it in there.'

They'd stopped outside what appeared to be a ruined cottage. It was in darkness. The men walked Perinne over to the building and led her inside. She could barely see but could hear the chip, chip, chipping and sparks of steel against flint as one of the men tried to light tinder. At last he succeeded and a candle soon cast a dim light about a small room. Perinne couldn't tell if this were a house or a simple farm building. There was a pile of rags in one corner and only a table and a small stool. There was no fireplace and it looked as though there'd been a fire in the middle of the room. Another small door stood across from the one they'd entered.

'Sit down,' the man with the pistol said. The other man produced a bag from a corner of the room and took out a flagon. 'Give her a drink. Watch her. I'll take the coach.' He left and the next thing Perinne heard were the horses galloping away.

'Take me home!'

'Be quiet.'

'*Non*! I want to go home, you cannot keep me here!'

'Sit still or I'll tie you up!'

'What is it that you want? You are not a servant at Cliff House. My papa is here. He will find me!'

'Quiet!'

'Mr Clarke! Mr Clarke!'

James Clarke was in the drawing room. He didn't tell the women that Will had said the man had a pistol.

'What is it, Joseph?'

'This letter, Mr Clarke, it were in the hall. It weren't there before.' James took the letter from Joseph. It wasn't sealed. It was addressed to *Sir Charles Tarrant*.

'What is it, Clarke?' Lady Elizabeth looked fearful. 'Open it!'

James opened the letter and read it to himself. 'It's er ... it's a ransom note, your ladyship.'

Jane Menniere stood up. 'What does it say? Let me see it. She took the note, looked at it then handed it back.

'What do they want?' Lady Elizabeth demanded.

Before James could answer the drawing room door was thrown open and Lucy came running in.

'Mr Clarke, Danny's back!'

## Chapter 18

# Where is Perinne?

The late coach pulled into the George. The ostler came out to take it to the back and unharness the horses. The coachman and landlord lifted trunks off the back. Two ladies gathered parcels and left for the street. A well-dressed man said he'd written the previous week and could his trunk be sent to his room. He asked what was going on - there were a great number of men and horses about.

'Sit him by the fire, Susan, and warm him some milk.' James Clarke dashed over to his son. Jack had appeared and was sitting next to his brother.

'He were in the ice 'ouse, I 'eard someone shoutin',' Will explained.

'Thank goodness you did!'

Like Will, Danny could say little about the man with the pistol. He didn't mention that he thought he knew some of the voices. He'd better not mention the feet either. His father had told him off about making fun of people and maybe it wasn't Millar. He sipped at the milk. Susan had given Will a cup too. They sat quietly.

Suddenly, the sound of horses broke the silence. Jack got up and went out into the courtyard. Through the window the boys could see Sir Charles, Edmund and another man who must be Perinne's father. Scott was also there and he dismounted first, followed by the others. Jack took two horses and Scott led the other two. Sir Charles came into the kitchen. Jack had told them that Danny had been found.

'How's the boy? Does either of them know anything?'

'They don't know who they were, Sir Charles,' James replied. 'I've asked Millar to find out whose coach is missing, he hasn't come back yet.'

'Go and check on your mother, Edmund.' Edmund grunted and left the room.

'I've roused the constable and Captain Palmer's sent word to rally some Dragoons,' Sir Charles said.

'I need to speak with you and Monsieur Menniere,' said James, indicating with his eyes that he wanted them to leave the room.

'What's that about?' Danny whispered to Will.

Will hunched his shoulders. Lucy came into the room with a tray.

'Lucy! What's going on?' Danny said, still whispering. 'Why does my father need to speak with Sir Charles?'

'It's probably about the letter.' The boys looked at each other. 'A letter was found.' Lucy explained. 'Askin' for a ransom, it is!'

'Money?' Will asked.

'I don't know. Oh, I'm so worried 'bout Miss Perinne. What have you boys got her mixed up in?'

'Us?' Danny gulped.

'I know she's been seein' ye both, I've a good mind to tell the master it's you two. How did them villains know where to grab her. You two coaxed her out to that coach, *that's* what ye did.' Lucy had tears in her eyes.

'No, Lucy, it ain't us, we don't know who 'as 'er,' Will

pleaded. 'There must be someone 'ere involved. Is there anyone new?'

'No, we've all been here years. Well, but for ...'

'But for who?' Danny asked.

'But for the coachman, he's new, Millar is.'

As the boys were about to speak again, James Clarke came back into the room.

'I've asked Scott to take you home. You too, Will, I won't take no for an answer this time. Straight to bed Danny and tell your mother Jack and I probably won't be back until late. Now go.'

The boys climbed into the coach. 'Let's meet tomorrow morning, Will, at the coppice. We've got to find Perinne. Ask Beth if she knows anything. Ask if she's heard of Millar.'

'I don't think she'll know 'bout 'im,' said Will. 'But I 'ave an idea who might do.'

'So, they want the boxes we have in return for Perinne.' Sir Charles paced up and down, shaking the letter in the air. 'Who left this James? Who?'

'It has to be one of the guests, or a servant, sir.'

'None of mine I hope.' Sir Charles's face reddened.

'The Lord himself knows why the children were in that coach. If there's bother, my son seems to be a part of it,' James added.

'Well, at least he's safe. They were after Perinne. They soon got rid of Daniel and the other boy. I can't think of any of the guests being involved. Did you find out whose coach it was?'

'No, Millar still hasn't returned. He's a strange one if I may say so. '

'But a good horseman, James, they can be hard to come by. Well, I'll go and check on Madame Menniere. Not much of a welcome for Yves to have his daughter snatched. Get some rest, James we'll check how the search is going on at first light. And another thing, I've ordered riding officers to search cellars in every inn. We could find the boxes they have before they get to ours!'

Edmund left his mother and the other women and went to his room. He pulled back the curtain and peered through the window. Most of the guests had left. Then he saw a faint light. It was a coach approaching. 'That's strange, it must have been sent for,' he thought. He watched as Millar, rather than a footman, stepped forward. He opened the door and pulled down the steps. A man then appeared from the house, limping and using a stick. It was the pale man. He said something to Millar and seemed to be shaking his head. Then he waved his free hand dismissively at Millar and climbed into the coach.

Will asked John Scott to leave him at the end of the old Bargate. There wasn't much room to take a coach down to his cottage, he told him. But the main reason was that he didn't want to go home just yet, despite the shocks of the night. He thanked Scott and waited until he was out of sight. He made his way back to the High Street. Candlelight flickered from windows and lamps cast a warm glow onto the road, brightening the night. There were plenty of people about. Some were laughing and joking, unaware of the drama just a few miles away, not knowing the danger Perinne was in. It was late, Beth was probably still at the George. He peered in at the Ship and other alehouses as he walked through the town. Will recognised some of the riding officers. He expected they were helping to look for Perinne. It had started to rain but before long he found who he was looking for.

'Isaac! Isaac!'

'Will lad!'

'Isaac, can I buy ye an ale?'

Despite being drunk Isaac chuckled. 'I can't let a young lad buy me ale!'

'I saw ye at Cliff House this mornin', sorry ye didn't get work.'

'Ye went yerself then, Will?'

'Yes, met a friend o' yours.'

'Did ye? Who's that then?'

'Said 'is name were Millar.'

Isaac jolted. 'Why was he asking about him?' he thought to himself. 'Millar? Don't know a Millar,' Isaac pretended, shaking his head.

'A coachman,' Will urged, 'friend of Adam Litty!' Will was guessing now but he'd seen Isaac's face change. He was sure that he could get him to say where Millar lived.

'Ah! Millar. Don't like 'im. Don't mess wi' 'im Will, lad.'

'Why? I've never seen 'im before. Does he live 'round 'ere?'

'Nah. But I 'eard he had a place out by Goddings Croft, or closer to Hinton way. Leave 'im well alone Will.'

Perinne watched the man. He was sitting at the old dusty table. There was a tray upon which the flagon from the bag stood. He reached and lifted it, pouring what looked like beer into a small cup. They've planned this, she thought.

'Here, drink this.' He passed her the cup, then put the flagon to his lips and drank. Perinne was thirsty but sipped at the beer. It could make her sleepy and she wanted to stay awake. There was no point trying to escape now. It was too dark and she could end up anywhere. She looked up at the roof, drips of water had started to fall. It had begun to rain. She would try at first light, but how with the man watching over her?

She tried not to sleep but must have dozed. When she opened her eyes the man was awake. The room was lighter, it must be dawn. She'd expected the second man to have returned but there was no sign of him. Looking around, the room appeared as if nothing had been there for some time. Also, the sacks where she'd been sitting were on straw, made like a bed. The man had earlier lit a fire, but it had gone out now. Beside the ashes was a small three-legged stool. The man had tried to light the fire again but had complained that the wood was wet. She needed to take a look outside.

'I need the necessary.'

'Hold it!'

'No! I need to go.'

The man glared at Perinne through the dim light.

'I will not run away.'

'I'll soon 'ave ye back if ye do! An' then I'll tie ye up!'

Perinne moved towards the small door at the back of the room. The man got up and followed her. 'I'll be by the door. I'll come and get ye if ye're more than a minute!'

Outside the sky was still and cloudless and daylight was appearing to her right. The rain had stopped and the dawn smelled damp. A low mist hung on the field close by. The cottage was on a single track. Perinne could see other buildings but couldn't make out what they were. They were too far away to attract attention though maybe somewhere to run to for help, but how could she be sure anyone lived there? She could hear the man and decided it would be better to wait and choose her chance to escape carefully.

She made her way back into the cottage and sat on the pile of sacks, pulling the blanket around her shoulders against the chill of the morning. She looked at the man who was now standing by the entrance at the front. He appeared strange with the mask still covering part of his face.

'What is your name?'

'Ye think I'm so stupid as to tell ye that?'

'What do you want? Money? My father has no money. This is why my mother and I have come to England.' It was a lie, but Perinne couldn't think why else she'd been snatched.

'Pah! Money! You folks have all the money, we poor do all the work!'

'What is your work?'

'What's that to you? Going to give me work are ye?'

'So, if you do not want money, why are you keeping me here? Take me back to Cliff House!'

'I can't do that.'

'Then how long shall I be here?'

'Look, miss, keep quiet. I'm just doin' as I've been bid, all right?'

Danny couldn't sleep. The rain was beating down on the thatch above him like pebbles on a drum. Everything was spinning in his head. How had the smugglers known they were going to be in the coach? Millar was involved. He had to tell his father, but he would see what Will said first. Danny's thoughts drifted. If they found out where Millar lived they could go and see if Perinne were there. And if they found Perinne they wouldn't be in any trouble, in fact they'd be heroes. Then he thought about her being hidden in the Forest, probably alone. 'Poor Perinne,' he thought. 'She must be feeling terrified.' There were so many places she could be hidden. It was going to be an almost impossible task to find her.

He turned over in his bed, lying one way then another, thinking it over again and again. The pale man was involved too. Everything seemed so complicated. Then Danny had an awful thought. The man in the coach with the pistol, what if it was Tom Pike! Just who has kidnapped Perinne? He remembered how his mother hadn't believed her ears when he'd told her about the night's events. Luckily she said he didn't need to go to church in the morning. He and Will had to go and look for Perinne. They'd agreed to meet at the coppice at eight o'clock. It was coming light already, but there were two more hours to wait.

## Chapter 19

# The search

Meekwick Ginn was waiting. He'd left Cliff House shortly after the last of the other guests but hadn't gone home. He'd taken a room at the Eight Bells. He thought Millar had been clever with the coach, getting it back so quickly but then found out it was Pike's work. It meant that the girl couldn't be very far away, but he didn't care. That was down to the men. Just so long as Tarrant gave him what he needed she'd be fine. He felt in his waistcoat for his watch, but it wasn't there. He grunted. He must have dropped it getting the letter out without anyone seeing him. Where was Millar? He had to be patient, he knew Millar might find it difficult to get away but he hated waiting for people. But it had to be this way, Pike was a cunning one. It was nearly dawn before the tapping noise on the door stirred him from his thoughts. Ginn lifted himself out of the chair with the help of his stick.

'Who is it?' he whispered.

'Me, Millar.' Millar slipped into the room, pulling the door closed quietly behind him. He pulled at his sleeves and took off his wet coat, then removed his hat.

'Well? What's happening over there?'

'Tarrant's pullin' his weight. Dragoons are out. He's ordered all the cellars to be checked.'

'Ha! Looking for more than the girl then! Well they

won't find anything. A good job done, Millar.'

'Nearly thrown by those meddlin' lads, though it spared us gettin' her out o' the house.'

'The deed's done. You'll be well rewarded, once we have the goods. Are you any nearer finding out where he has those seven boxes hidden?'

'They're not at the house, I'm certain o' that now.'

Ginn slammed his fist on the wall. 'Damn Tarrant! This plan has to work out. Those boxes and that machine are mine!'

Beth said Adam Litty had been in the George most of the night. Nothing unusual had happened. The stage coach had arrived and a gentleman was staying in the rooms, but that was common too. Beth and his mother were still in bed when Will was up and about at first light.

'Well, Sam, how 'bout doing some sniffin' around?' Will rubbed the dog's ears. He opened the cupboard and saw a loaf of bread and a lump of cheese. Wrapping some in a cloth he put it into his pocket. He grabbed his coat and hat and set out. He'd probably be early, but then Perinne was out there somewhere. He'd barely slept for worry. Was it his fault? If they hadn't let Perinne become involved she might not have been snatched. But it was she who'd told them about the incredible machine. Is that what they wanted?

He made his way down the High Street again, this time with Sam at his heels. The few people who were about were wrapped up against the chilly morning. The sky was heavy with grey clouds, puddles were everywhere. It had rained again overnight and would probably come down again before too long. He reached the corner by the George and glanced towards the Priory. He noticed a figure coming out of the Eight Bells. Millar! Will ran across the road and hid behind one of the arches of the market area below the town hall. He poked his head around to watch where Millar went. If he were walking then he could follow him. But soon a boy appeared from around the end of the building leading a horse. Millar mounted the horse and set out. Will ducked back as Millar rode by and down Castle Street. 'Back to Cliff House or home?' thought Will. He left his hiding place and set out watching Millar ahead until he disappeared.

'Great! You've brought Sam.'

'Ye're early, Danny.'

'Couldn't sleep much. Did Beth see anyone?'

'Only Adam Litty. So it weren't 'im last night.'

'I've just seen Millar,' Danny said, 'he rode past me.'

'Aye, I saw 'im coming out of the Eight Bells. I wonder why Miller were there. It also means 'e's not at 'ome!'

'Do you think that's where Perinne is?'

'Don't know, but we 'ave to start somewhere, 'e lives out by Goddin's Croft or around there. Let's go!'

'But what if he's on his way home?'

'Let's see if we can find it first.'

The two made their way towards Burton. They left the track and decided to cross the fields so they wouldn't be seen. The land was flat and despite the ground being damp and muddy the boys moved as quickly as they could, keeping close to the hedges. They continued in silence. Occasionally they would disturb quails which scurried across the soil before flapping up in fright. The boys inched past farm buildings and skirted fields where cows were huddled together. After a while they could make out the cottages of Goddings Croft. Then they had a stroke of luck.

'Look, over there!' Will pointed at a shabby cottage set a short distance away from the others in the hamlet.

'What?'

'That 'orse! I'm sure it's Millar's!'

The boys crept towards the cottage. It was old and didn't look as though anyone lived there. They crouched down behind a hawthorn hedge. It gave them little cover but for a swathe of ivy and a few buds. The boys lay down and watched, ignoring the damp. Sam was lying by Will's side. The horse was tied to a low fence. It was definitely Millar's. Then the small door of the cottage opened. A man came out pulling off a face mask - it was Millar. Another man, masked, also appeared at the door. The boys couldn't make out what they were saying. Sam made a low growl.

'Shhh, Sam, shhh.' Will clasped his hand gently over the dog's nose.

They watched as Millar untethered the horse. He put the toe of his large foot into the stirrup and launched himself onto the horse's back. Then he turned and trotted along the muddy track towards the other cottages.

Danny turned to Will. 'What shall we do?'

'It's three against one.'

'We're going to go in?'

'Aye.'

'But what if there's more than one of them?

'Why would they 'ave two to watch one girl?'

'May have.'

'Let's see when we get there. I'm 'oping it's the same man as in the coach.'

'Why?'

'He were left 'anded.'

'What's that got to do with it?'

'Ye'll see.'

Danny shook his head, bewildered. 'How do we stop him coming after us?'

'We tie 'im up.'

'What with?'

Will knelt and unbuttoned his coat. Wrapped around his waist was a length of rope. In fact, when he unwound it Danny could see that there were two lengths.

'Will, that's great! But where do we go then? Millar could be in one of the other cottages.'

'We'll go back over the fields to your 'ouse, or to the Scott's if it's nearer!'

Danny had a sudden thought. 'No, I've a better idea. My uncle's house is over the field at Hinton, that's the nearest. Perinne will be safe there.'

'That's settled then.' Will squatted down. 'Now, this'll be what we do.'

The boys crept across the track towards the cottage. Danny stood at the side as instructed and Will edged around the back. The damp morning chill smarted Danny's cheeks. What was Will doing? Then a whisper sounded and Will's head appeared from around the wall of the cottage.

'Psss ... Danny, go.'

Danny nodded. He inched quietly to the front and stood by the door. His heart was pounding. Taking a deep breath, he knocked.

Inside Perinne was now sitting on the little stool. She was watching the man eat. She'd refused the food brought in by the visitor, Millar - she knew it was him despite the mask. Should she try to run now whilst he was off guard? Suddenly there was a knock at the door. The man turned. This was unexpected and Perinne could tell he was nervous, he started breathing heavily. He leaped to his feet, grabbed his pistols, pushing one into his belt and raised the other in readiness in his left hand. He moved over to the door. With his right hand he opened it as slowly as he could. He peered through the gap in the door but couldn't see anyone without opening the door any wider.

'Go away!' he growled.

At the same time, the door at the back of the room opened without a sound. Perinne was amazed to see Will slip quietly in followed by his dog. He lifted his finger to his lips. In his other hand he was holding a short, thick tree branch.

He lifted it.

'Now Danny!'

As the front door was pushed inwards Will brought the branch down onto the kidnapper's head. 'Run out, Perinne!' Will shouted. 'Wait by the front.'

The man squealed in pain. One hand instinctively went to hold his head, his other swiftly swinging the pistol around. He let off a shot which hit the ceiling bringing dirty straw tumbling down. But it was too late. The boys set upon him, sending him face down onto the floor. The pistol crashed out of his hand. Perinne jumped up from the stool and snatched the other pistol before the man could reach for it. Danny and Will were now sitting on the man's back. But the man was twisting from side to side trying to throw them off. Then he tried kicking his legs backwards. Sam, who'd been barking loudly, was now snarling and growling as his teeth gripped and tugged at the man's coat.

'Quiet!' Will had grabbed the loaded pistol from Perinne and was now holding it to the man's head. Danny looked at him, astonished that Will could handle the pistol with such ease. The man continued kicking and spitting.

'Varmints, ye devil's children!'

Will grabbed a dirty cloth from his pocket and pushed it into the man's mouth. Perinne was now sitting on the man's legs but struggled to keep them down as he tried to free himself.

Will then gave the pistol to Danny who'd shuffled down to help Perinne. Pulling the man's waving arms behind his back Will tied them together. He turned and smiled at Perinne.

'Are ye all right? Has 'e hurt ye?'

'No. He has not and I am all right,' she said, trying not to let Will hear the fear in her voice.

Still sitting on the man's back Will tightened the second piece of rope around the man's legs and around the leg of the table. Sam was now sniffing in the corner. Danny was shaking. He'd never held a pistol before.

'Point it at 'is 'ead,' Will shouted.

'What has the dog found?' Perinne asked.

Will shuffled to the corner and rummaged in some sacking on the floor. 'It's a watch! No, there's more! The rogue's a thief as well as a kidnapper. Come on, let's go!'

Will pushed the booty into his pocket. He and Perinne jumped up and rushed to the door. Danny was looking in horror at the man, who was writhing on the floor.

'Danny, come on. Quickly – and bring the pistol!'

Danny leaned down, he pulled the mask away. The man's eyes, wild and menacing from his pox-marked face, glared up at Danny. Tightly grasping the weapon, Danny turned and hurriedly followed Perinne and Will out of the door. The three ran across to the fields as fast as they could.

'Come on, this way!' Danny shouted, suddenly finding confidence.

It had started to rain again. They ran without stopping through mud and leaf-strewn thickets and by the time they reached Hinton they were wet and bedraggled. Danny led them to his uncle's house and flung the door open.

The three ran into the cottage panting for breath followed quickly by Sam who started barking.

'Danny! In the Lord's name, what's happened?'

'Father!'

'What on this earth!' James Clarke exclaimed. 'And a pistol! Give that to me, now!'

Mary Hewitt dashed over to Perinne throwing her shawl around the girl's shoulders. 'Oh, Miss Perinne, you're safe! But look at you! Your pretty dress all torn and those dancing slippers are ruined! Come with me. Let's see if we can find something dry for you to put on. You poor girl, what you must have been through,' Aunt Mary continued, shaking her head as she led Perinne up a narrow staircase.

'It's Millar, father, he's the one who took Perinne. And there's another man. We've tied him up and left him.'

James Clarke's face was wide-eyed, his mouth open in astonishment.

'I noticed Millar's feet, do you remember father? That's how I knew it was him carrying me to the ice house! Will found out where he lived and ...'

'Stop! Why didn't you come to Cliff House and tell us?'

'We wanted to find Perinne. Will found out where Millar lived, and ...'

'We *all* wanted to find her.' James Clarke's voice was raised and agitated. 'You put yourselves' and Perinne's lives in grave danger. You should have come to me!'

'But Will ...'

Will was standing next to Uncle John. He'd seen him before in town and he was sure it had been with Isaac.

'Perhaps, Will, you'd like to explain to me what you boys have been doing. Where is this man now?'

## Chapter 20

# A clue uncovered

Perinne followed Aunt Mary up the narrow staircase of the Hinton cottage. She was shaking and now that she was out of Will and Danny's sight, she allowed the tears welling in her eyes to roll down her face.

They turned into a little room and Aunt Mary put her arms around her. 'Come now, miss, ye safe now, an' we'll soon 'ave ye back with ye mother. I'm sure Sir Charles will catch the villains who did this to ye. Let's get ye out o' those wet things. It's a while since there were a young girl in this house.' Aunt Mary opened a trunk. 'Our Betsy were last to leave home, but I may 'ave something here you c'n wear. An' she ain't far away if we need to fetch somethin'.'

Perinne was shivering with cold. She wiped her damp face with the back of her hand, leaving a muddy streak on her cheek. Her hair was wet and the ribbons undone and tangled. She was tired now and wanted more than anything to be back at Cliff House. Aunt Mary rummaged and lifted garments to check the size. Next to the trunk something else was piled, it had a cloth draped over it. Perinne noticed the cloth had been pulled away a little. It was something wooden. There were letters showing - '*telot*' was on one side and '*ivé*' and '*atre*' were showing on other parts. Aunt Mary laid a dress over the pile and picked up a petticoat.

'Let's try this.'

Aunt Mary helped Perinne out of her wet dress and dried her as best she could. She pulled a muslin petticoat over the girl's head and leaned over to get the dress. Perinne watched as the cloth moved further. It was a box. There was more than one. Perinne could now see all the lettering on the biggest of the boxes. '*M Costelot,*', '*Privé*', '*Quatre*'- the same words as those Will had shown her. She thought back to the scrap of paper, *Treize,* thirteen, the thirteenth box. And these had to be some of the missing boxes! How many were there?

'You all right, Miss, ye look as though ye've seen a ghost? We need to get ye home. The dress is a bit big, but it'll do for now. Come on then.'

Mary pulled an old shawl from the trunk and wrapped it around Perinne's shoulders. She picked up the wet, muddy dress, quickly wrapped it in a cloth and handed it to the girl. They went downstairs. Will and Danny weren't there so they walked to the door. Outside Uncle John was sitting on a trap which had a single pony harnessed to its wooden struts. Will was by his side and Sam was sitting quietly next to the pony. Danny was on a horse with his father. Both boys had blankets wrapped around them against the weather.

'Come on, Miss Perinne,' James said. 'Let's get you back to Cliff House.'

Perinne climbed onto the cart and sat between Uncle John and Will. She leaned over and whispered in Will's ear. Will's eyes widened and his mouth fell open with shock. Before he could speak it was Perinne's turn to lift her finger to her lips.

When Millar arrived back at Cliff House Sir Charles and Yves Menniere were out looking for Perinne.

He stamped into the kitchen

'So, the shoot's been cancelled?' he snarled.

Joseph was by the range. 'Aye, Master says to have the overnight guests' coaches ready for going after breakfast. It's late. Everyone who's able's out lookin' for Miss Perinne.'

'Everyone? Where's Scott?'

'Scott's been sent to town to get Dr Quartley. Madame Menniere is most disturbed. Lucy's helpin' her Ladyship sit with her.'

'Is Master Edmund with the searchers?'

'Aye, he's out too.'

Millar grunted and stormed back outside. Susan shrugged her shoulders. 'He don't seem worried much about the goin's on.'

Joseph shook his head. 'Strange character, that one Susan.'

'Well, we've got to get on, Joseph. A meal still has to be served to the guests, can't be havin' all this food wasted. Though whether folks'll feel like eatin' I'm not so sure.'

Joseph walked over to the window. 'Look! Susan, come here, quickly!'

'Well, the Lord 'ave mercy on us! It's Mr Clarke. Is that young Danny with him?'

'Look who's on the cart, Susan, it's Miss Perinne. Send one o' the maids to tell the mistress!'

Susan dashed to the dining room where the remaining servants were preparing the table. Joseph was now running across the gravel of the courtyard. James stopped and Danny leaned over to be helped off the horse. Perinne climbed down from the trap.

'Let us meet on Monday afternoon, Will, at the beach,' she whispered.

Jane Menniere had now appeared at the rear door. 'Perinne!'

Perinne waved her hand. She looked up at Danny's Uncle John. 'Thank you, Mr Hewitt, and please say thank you to Mrs Hewitt for helping me.'

'Our pleasure, Miss Perinne, now go on or ye'll catch a cold.'

She smiled and then smiled at Danny, who had come over to join Will. James Clarke had dismounted from his horse. Ben, the stable boy, appeared and led the horse away. Uncle John turned the trap around and set off with Will and Danny, Sam scampering alongside them.

Jane Menniere was now holding Perinne, her eyes brimming with tears of relief. 'Oh, thank you Clarke.'

'It's the boys you need to be thanking, Ma'am,' James replied. 'Please look to Miss Perinne. Then I expect Sir Charles will want to question her on his return as to who these rogues were. The boys have told me what they know.' He then turned to Joseph. 'Have you seen Millar here today?' he asked him.

'Aye, Mr Clarke, he were in the kitchen a while since, then went off. To the coach house I think.'

As James Clarke strode across the courtyard, the stable door opened and out rode Millar.

'Millar! Stop!'

James ran to find his horse, but Ben had already unsaddled it.

Will curled the blanket around his shoulders and pulled down his hat. The wind was blowing into his face and the rain tapped on his cheeks. Uncle John was concentrating on driving the trap. His silver hair was hanging wet down the back of his coat. He'd said nothing whilst travelling to Cliff House nor since they'd left for Burton to take Danny home. Now, as they made their way to town Will wondered if he could get Uncle John to say anything about the boxes he was storing. It was almost certain that they were being looked after for Sir Charles. As they reached the main road into Christchurch, Sam barked. A group of red-coated Dragoons were approaching them from the north.

'Probably coming back from checking the Forest,' Uncle John spoke at last.

'They'll all need to be called in now,' Will replied. Apart from the rattle of the trap's wheels the two sat in silence again. The rain had stopped. Sam was ahead of them, sniffing at shrubs. Then Uncle John said something that took Will by surprise.

'I knew ye father, Will. He were a good man. How is it you know our Danny?'

Will explained how they'd first met on the quayside. 'I'd 'eard shots on the marsh and Danny's brother Jack had 'eard 'em and then Edmund Tarrant attacked him. We decided to find out what's goin' on.'

'An' 'ave ye?'

Will wasn't going to answer that. 'How did ye know me father?'

'I expect ye know Isaac Hooper?'

'Isaac? Aye! He's a neighbour o' ours.'

'We were at sea together. They were tough years an' we saw some sights we did. We both got tired o' wanderin' the oceans. Danny's father got me work on the estate. I take this old trap down to town on occasion and meet up wi' Isaac, that's 'ow I met ye father.' Then I found work a bit nearer 'ome. Keeps a roof o'er our 'eads.'

As Uncle John turned the trap into Purewell a horse heading from town reared up.

'Whose is that damned hound!'

Will's heart sank, it was Sir Charles and Edmund was

with him. Some of the footmen who he'd been with the night before were also there on horseback.

'Come 'ere Sam, here!'

'You!' Edmund rode over to the trap. 'It's that ruffian again, father.'

'This ruffian, as ye call 'im, 'as just rescued Miss Perinne!' Uncle John cut in.

Sir Charles nudged his boots into his stallion and trotted over to the trap. 'Perinne is found? Where? Where is she now? Is she well?'

'Aye, she were at a ruin at Goddin's Croft. An' now she's safe, thanks to this fellow an' my nephew,' Uncle John beamed.

'Well, young man, first Daniel and now Perinne.'

'It's too good to be true father. He's probably part of the plot!'

'Quiet, Edmund! You're John Hewitt are you not?'

'Aye, Sir Charles, they ran to our house, James Clarke was with us er ..., as ye may know. Miss Perinne's back at Cliff House and I'm just takin' young Will 'ere back 'ome. They've all 'ad a shock.'

'Well, Will, it seems we've a lot to thank you for. I'll need to ask you some questions I think.'

'I've explained all what 'appened to Mr Clarke, Sir.' Will didn't want to go back to Cliff House now. He was cold, wet and hungry.

'Well, we can always send for you,' Sir Charles replied. 'Buckle, go back and have the Mayor call off the search. Newton, go and let Captain Palmer know.'

Two footmen turned their horses and rode back towards the town.

'Well done, young man.' Sir Charles kicked again and his horse set off at a gallop.

'Keep that dog away from the horses! People like you shouldn't keep dogs!' Edmund sneered, dug his heels into his horse and set off after his father.

'Don't worry, Will lad, Edmund Tarrant's ne'er been gi'en any manners.'

The trap pulled up outside Will's cottage. Meg Gibbs appeared at the door.

'What's happened, Will? Is everything all right?' She looked at her son and then at the driver.

'John? John Hewitt! Well, bless my soul!'

'Hello there, Meg, ye've a brave lad 'ere. William'd be proud o' what the lad's done.'

'Will? What 'ave ye been doin?'

'A proper hero, that's what 'e is!'

'Come on in then Will, let's hear all about it! Hope ye'll join us John.'

An hour later Millar jumped off his horse and handed the stable boy a farthing.

'Wait here!' he demanded. He strode around to the entrance of the Eight Bells. He found Meekwick Ginn sitting in a dark corner.

'So, you're back. What's going on?'

'The girl's free! They know it's me. I have to get away or Tarrant'll make sure of a rope around my neck. I need my pay.'

'Where's Pike?'

'I found him tied up at the cottage.'

'Is he harmed? Who was it freed her, Tarrant?'

'Nah, kids.'

'What? Pah! The man's weakened; he's only been out of gaol a week! There's no pay for you, you've failed Millar! Get out of my sight!'

Millar grabbed Ginn by the coat and pulled him up until their faces met. Ginn baulked at Millar's foul breath. His chair tumbled backwards and knocked the tables. Tankards fell clattering onto the stone floor.

'It was Pike's idea to kidnap the girl, so don't blame me! Do ye want me to let Tarrant know ye were behind this and where the damned boxes are? Pay me now!'

The landlord dashed over to break the two apart.

'All right, all right. But I never want to see you again, Millar, or you'll regret it! Now let me go!'

Ginn sighed with relief, reached into his pocket and took out a purse. 'Here, begone!'

Millar snatched the money and stormed out of the alehouse.

Grandpa was resting in his usual chair with Sarah by his side playing with Dilly. Danny was sitting in his favourite place looking out over the fields. He was now cleaned up and in fresh clothes. He was trying to read but couldn't concentrate. The morning's events had startled him. Last night had been bad enough. But his biggest worry was Will. He'd only known him a week, he didn't really know him at all. He was amazed at the way he'd held the pistol, as easily as the kidnapper had. Will hadn't spoken on the way home other than to say that Perinne had something to tell him. They'd agreed to meet at Muddiford on Monday afternoon and now he had to decide whether or not to go.

## Chapter 21

# Where are all the boxes?

'Well, James, this is a turn of affairs. The three children have obviously made good friends. Those boys are heroes. But it doesn't tell us where those seven boxes are.'

Sir Charles Tarrant was sitting behind his desk drumming his fingers on the green leather top.

'Can you meet with Sir George today?'

'Yes, sir.'

'Good. The other thing of concern is who left the ransom note.'

'The boys said that one of the men who took Miss Perinne was in servant's livery. Millar will have arranged that. Maybe there was more than one of them.'

Sir Charles sighed. 'It's the only answer. The guests are my friends. How is your boy? I can't believe what those two did, James.'

'I'm in two minds, sir. Proud, of course, but in heaven's name they could all have been killed. We've no idea about these rogues. Thankfully Danny seems well enough, back at school tomorrow. That should take his mind off things.'

'He's at the free grammar school?'

'Yes, he is.'

'Then maybe we should see about sending him to board.'

'Yes, sir, but ...'

'As a reward. And this other boy, is he at school or has he a trade?'

'He mends nets and helps on the fishing boats. His father's dead. He lives with his mother and sister in town.'

'Perhaps an apprenticeship can be found for him. Mr Clingan's Trust could help. Now, to the matter in hand. Any news from the town?'

James shook his head. 'No, they didn't find anything searching the cellars. I've had people listening out. Nothing of substance, but I'm sure the other boxes are still in Christchurch, somewhere.'

'And what about this escaped prisoner?'

'Tom Pike?' James Clarke hunched his shoulders. 'He wasn't in town when the goods were brought in. He hasn't been seen - in hiding I expect - though not sure I'd recognise him.'

'Keep looking, James. I need all the machine's parts, especially now Yves is here. I think you may go now and see to that boy of yours. I've got dinner with the guests and later, hopefully, a few hands of cards with the Duchess.'

'So, John Hewitt, how's that wife o' yours?' Meg handed some tea to her visitor. It was a very rare occasion that they had tea to drink. Isaac was usually the source of supply, trying to gain favour using the spoils of a night's work. Will finished his cup. He loved the warmth of the liquid sliding down his throat. Also, it was Sunday and they might even have some meat today. As his mother and John chatted, he climbed up the stepladder to the attic room to change. He really wanted to bathe. The river would be too cold, but his clothes had dried and smelled awful. There was no sign of Beth. Will could hear his mother and John Hewitt laughing in the room below. He'd brought his coat with him and felt in the pocket, bringing out the things he'd taken from the kidnapper. There were two gold watches and a silver snuff box. Both watches had white faces and Roman numbers. One had a case and on it the letters M and G were engraved. The other was very ornately decorated with swirls of leaves. The snuff box was also engraved and filled with the brown powder. He put the things behind his bed with the box. He lifted off his dirty shirt. His eyes felt heavy and, pulling his blanket over his shoulders, Will lay down on his bed and fell into a deep sleep.

Perinne enjoyed her second warm bath in as many days. Lucy chatted to her, but all she could think about was her escape from the men.

'An' Joseph said it weren't money they were after, miss.'

'*Pardon?*'

'The ransom. There were a letter, but Joseph said that it wasn't money they were after.'

'Then what was it that they wanted?'

'Don't know, miss.'

'Than I shall ask papa.'

'You must be so excited he's here.'

'Did you know that he was coming, Lucy?'

'No, Miss. There, all nice and clean. Now into bed. Dr Quartley says you must rest.'

James Clarke rode past the end of the road leading to his home and continued into Christchurch. He wouldn't be needed at Cliff House again until the morning. His letter had been answered and Sir George Cook would be at the George. His horse's hooves clomped on the wooden bridge. People were about, wrapped up against the March winds. Ladies were holding their long skirts and their bonnets were tied securely under their chins. He rode by the Customs Officer's little thatched cottage. He might not need to take the visitor there tomorrow, but he was as frustrated as Sir Charles. Who had funded the gang to bring in the stolen machine? Where were these boxes? And now Yves Menniere was here to take the machine to London, though maybe not now Sir George had arrived. He crossed the ancient bridge and glanced over to the old house and ruined castle. The sun had come out from behind the dark clouds and lit up the Priory where a bell was tolling. James loved his town. The people were good. Many of the smugglers were just ordinary men wanting to feed their families. But he wanted more for his family and was proud of what he'd achieved. And now Sir Charles seemed to be offering Danny a chance to go to a boarding school. But what about Jack? It wouldn't be fair for one boy to have such an advantage and not the other.

He rode into the yard of the George where a stable boy appeared and took his horse. Inside people were sitting holding tankards of beer. Some had long white pipes in their mouths. The smell of tobacco mixed with smoke from a fire burning in the grate, was giving off a nutty smell. A man threw a log onto the fire. It must have been damp as it spat and crackled. By the bowed window a well-dressed man stood up as James ducked his head and entered the small room.

'James Clarke? Good afternoon. Sir George Cook.' The man held out his hand to James. He had short, dark hair greying at the sides, framing a long face. His clothes were of good quality. 'This is quite a town. The coachman said there was a prisoner on the loose hereabouts, and there's talk about a missing girl.'

'Yes, sir, no word of the prisoner, but the girl is Jane and Yves Menniere's daughter, Sir Charles's niece. She's back at Cliff House now, thank our Lord.' James sat down.

'And was it connected to our problem?'

James lowered his voice to a whisper. 'Yes, there was a ransom note. They wanted the shipment in return for the girl.'

'Do we know who they are yet?'

'No.' James shook his head. He explained how Perinne had been rescued by Will and Danny. George Cook gave a great belly laugh.

'Sorry, James, this must have been a shock to you, but you have to admire the boys. Maybe we should get them to investigate the missing boxes!'

'We'd have to tell Danny *not* to do so. He generally does the opposite of what he's asked these days!'

'Well, let's go for a walk. I don't wish to go into detail about this in such a public place. And I have a confession to make.'

The two men rose. Cook, who was as tall as James Clarke, put on his coat and picked up his tricorn hat, placing it firmly on his head. Both left the George, making their way towards the Priory.

Cook began, 'As you know, my friend was at Cliff House the day after the shipment came in. Sir Charles had told him about it, hoping he knew of someone who could build the machine. When he told me what it was, I thought it too important just to be sold, especially something of use to our armies. But the idea is so incredible we fear people will think it a conjuring trick.'

James nodded in agreement. 'You do know that Sir Charles has a buyer in London, a contact of Yves Menniere? They are to split the money.'

'Yes, I did know. Well, that's changed. There's a man of science, a Frenchman, living in America, Boston in fact. We think he can make this machine work, then it will be even more valuable. If we can get the parts together and out of Poole to Newfoundland, he can arrange things from there.'

The two had reached the Quay where fishing boats were being cleaned after a day's toil. Gulls were swooping and screeching and ducks glided along the glistening water.

'The Royal Society has a new home. New wonders and inventions are exciting and this is no different, but we've kept it quiet. Just my friend and I are aware of it. Plus whoever it is the machine was stolen for. But if this machine works, James, just imagine how the world would change and it needs to be in our hands, not those of our enemies.'

'The Society will fund this work?'

Cook shook his head. 'No, this is my confession. I haven't mentioned it. I did think about talking to Gustavus Brander, he's a Fellow of the Society, he lives here in Christchurch, but he's away. Do you know him?

'I know of him. He's visited Cliff House on occasion.'

'Well, I fear the Society members will think the whole thing too incredulous. I'll pay. And pay Charles Tarrant if I have to.'

'What if the machine doesn't work?'

'Then few will be the wiser will they? I don't want to be made a fool of, especially if it's just a man's fancy.'

The two walked back towards the Priory. People were gathering for the Sunday service. They stopped at the church porch. 'I'll go to see the Chief Riding Officer tomorrow, try to get the names of some local venturers, it may give us some clues about where to look next. Can you get to town and meet me again? Leave it a day - how about Tuesday night?'

'Yes, Sir George, about seven o'clock?'

The two men lifted their hats. Cook nodded. 'Good day, James.' He turned and went into the church.

Isaac had followed the two men from the George. He was now behind a yew tree, watching. He'd been told that the one in the tricorn hat had arrived in town on Saturday night and the other was one of Sir Charles's men. A girl had been kidnapped and Meekwick Ginn had been about too. The search for the girl had stirred up the town but no one knew what it was all about. Adam Litty wouldn't speak to him, but why was young Will asking about John Millar, why would he want to know about him? Millar was a newcomer and no friend of Adam Litty. In fact, thought Isaac, he's a friend of no one around here.

Edmund was angry - angry the shoot had been cancelled because of the stupid French girl. He was angry too that the Clarke boy and that town fisher boy were being made out to be heroes. She was back now, so why couldn't they go shooting? He aimed his gun at a pigeon that had settled on the bough of an oak tree just coming into bud. The bang of the gunpowder startled the bird. It flew away before the shot hit it. 'Why would anyone want to kidnap her?' he thought. He reloaded the gun. 'I went out last night on the search.' The crack of the second shot shattered the silence. 'Why isn't father ever pleased with me?' A shot blasted into the air again, smoke framing Edmund's frowning face. He'd get his own back on those two boys.

## Chapter 22

# A good deed turns sour

Will most often woke in darkness. There were no windows in the attic room. When he climbed down the steps into the main room, dawn was creeping into the cottage, so it was around six. He'd slept soundly after the events of Sunday. He wondered how Danny was, he'd looked in shock holding the pistol at the kidnapper, but there'd been no choice. And Perinne, he'd never known a girl who'd get herself involved in a fight like she had, but she must have been terrified. The wind was blowing wildly outside. He drank some water and ate some bread and pulled on his coat. Walking to the Quay, Will could smell the breweries were already at work, the bakers too. He liked the early mornings, but there were lots of things on his mind. He'd meet with Danny and Perinne later, if they could both get away. Maybe they could piece together more about what had happened. He also needed to take the watches and snuff box to Cliff House. First, though, he needed to see if there was any work for him today. When he reached the Quay the *Solomon* was being tossed around on the choppy water. Master Hardyman was on the deck but none of the other hands were around.

'Sorry, Will, I'm not takin' her out. I'll go on the next tide this afternoon if this wind drops. But ye won't be needed. Sorry, lad.'

Will nodded. That decided it. He'd go home for the stolen things then on to Cliff House. Maybe there'd be a reward. That would make up for losing wages.

Beth was in the kitchen when he returned. The fire he'd lit earlier was now burning nicely. Sam had found his way inside and was curled up in front of it. A kettle hanging above it was steaming.

'No work, brother?'

'No, too windy and the nets are done. Where's mother?'

'She's still abed. She was up 'til late talkin' to John Hewitt. I hear you're a hero!' Beth smiled and handed her brother a cup of hot, but very weak tea.

'Tea again?' Will lifted the cup, holding it in both hands to warm them.

'Left over from last night, it's the last until Isaac finds mother some more. So, what are you goin' to do today?'

'Goin' up to Cliff House. That kidnapper was a thief too. Sam found some loot. I'm takin' the things back. Might get a reward.'

'There was a lot of talk about the girl in the George last night. Dragoons searched all the cellars. Every place searched, folks said.'

'Perinne. The girl, 'er name's Perinne. She's a friend. I've told ye before.'

'I know, and you're her rescuer,' Beth laughed. 'We are gettin' friendly with the gentry, aren't we now?'

Will ignored his sister. 'Have ye 'eard anythin' else?'

'No.'

'No strangers?'

'It's a coachin' inn, Will, we have strangers comin' all the time. We've a gentleman stayin. He's a *Sir*. Sir George

Cook.' Beth laughed again. 'Ye not the only one mixin' with the Lords an' Ladies.'

The wind continued to bluster as Will set out for Cliff House. He would ask for Danny's father, or maybe John Scott. Hunched against the gusts which were whistling around him Will put his hands in his pockets. He could feel the watches and the snuff box. Maybe he should have kept them. But Danny and Perinne had seen them. His father often told him to take what comes to him. His father had also taught him to hunt. He could trap and bait. His father hadn't been sure about school, but his mother wanted Will and Beth to learn to read and write. Then all that had to be forgotten. When his father lay dying he'd told him, 'Will, it's up to you now to take care o' ye mother and sister.' Will had made the promise and he wanted to try to keep it at all costs. As he approached the road to Burton he thought of Danny. He was lucky going to school. And Perinne probably had a governess. 'I will learn to read and write,' he thought to himself. 'Then I can find a better job. I could be a merchant or run an inn. Yes, run an inn, like the George.'

Will daydreamed all the way to the gates. He continued along the pathway where just two days ago he'd helped to cut the grass. He could see the entrance to the courtyard ahead. The coaches seemed to have gone. As he approached he could see the one that had brought the Duchess and her daughter was still there.

'Halt! You! Stop!'

'Oh *no*, not again,' Will sighed.

'Get off our land, lout.'

'I'm here to see ye father.'

Edmund was with his two pals Adam and Simon who'd been at the beach last week. 'He's not here, go away.'

'Then I'll see Mr Clarke.' Will walked on past them.

'Clarke? A servant? You may speak to me instead.'

'No.' Will quickened his pace.

'What? You can't say no to me. You must do as I say on our land. Come here.'

One of Edmund's friends started laughing.

'Enough!' he yelled at them. 'Come back here, town boy.'

Will knew he couldn't fight all three alone. His best chance was to run to the house. He set off at a sprint. The ground was slippery with mud churned up by the coaches and horses over the weekend. His foot slid in a rut and he tumbled over.

'Get him!' Edmund shouted.

Simon held Will to the ground and began to punch him. Will curled up, shielding his head with his arm as best he could.

'You too,' Edmund ordered Adam who'd stepped back.

Then the silver snuff box fell from Will's pocket.

'Look!' Simon shouted.

Edmund stooped and picked up the box. 'What's this? Have you been thieving, ruffian?'

'My name's Will, and nay, I 'aven't.'

'Get up,' Edmund ordered. 'Search him.'

'There's more!' Simon lifted the two watches.

'Give them to me,' Edmund ordered. 'Quite a treasure trove! Go on, get off our land.'

Will was wet and covered in mud. There was no point in arguing. This day was turning into a disaster. He had another shirt but no more breeches until the ones from Sunday were dried. His coat was filthy now.

Will picked up his hat which had blown off in the scuffle and walked away, kicking at a stone. 'Why should Edmund Tarrant get away with this?' he thought. 'Danny and Perinne knew the truth.' Maybe he could ask Danny to explain things to his father. He'd reached the gate when he heard a noise from behind him. He turned. It was Edmund's friend, the one who'd stood back. He was riding a small Forester pony, like Perinne's.

'Stop, Will.'

Will continued. He was in no mood for another fight, even if it was one-against-one.

'Stop, please.'

Will took a deep breath and turned. 'What do ye want? To beat me again?'

'No. I've come away. I can't abide Edmund anymore. I'm going home.'

'Well good for ye.' Will turned and walked on.

'Wait, please. Let me travel with you. I'm Adam,' the boy said. The little pony started to trot to keep up with Will's fast pace. 'I've seen you in town. My father's the vicar.'

'Never seen ye other than last week,' Will said.

'I go to boarding school but we're home for Easter. What does your father do?'

'He's dead.'

'Sorry.'

Will had pushed his hat back onto his head, his hair bobbing along his back as he started to run.

'I'm sorry, Will. Please. I wish I hadn't thumped you at the beach last week.'

'Feelin' guilty I 'ope.' Will turned again to look at Adam.

'Yes. Yes, I am. I only know Edmund and Simon. I've no other friends. I was afraid they'd leave me out if I didn't do as Edmund said.'

'Then yer a fool.'

'Do you think I could be your friend and that other boy's?' Adam pulled the reins of his little pony and watched as Will got further and further away.

As Will reached the town there were lots of people about. Market day had come around again with animals in the pens, straw blowing around and people selling meats, vegetables and other goods. Women were carrying their purchases in baskets made from the local bullrushes. He stopped just past the old bridge and looked over to the Priory. Life wasn't fair. It was his own fault, he'd prayed for a bit of excitement in his life but he was still getting the rough end of it all. He was feeling hungry but had no money with him to buy food. He wondered what time it was. He could visit Beth in the George and she might give him some broth or something. But how could he, covered in mud?

'Will, please, I'm really sorry.'

Will turned. He hadn't heard Adam step up beside him. He was now walking and leading the pony. Adam's face looked pale. His fair hair curled out from under his hat. It was similar to Danny's, he thought. 'Edmund's father'll find out the truth 'bout those watches,' Will said.

'Yes. Edmund's stupid. It wouldn't cross his mind that you wouldn't be going to the house if you weren't returning them.'

'Listen, Adam, I need to get 'ome. I'm filthy.'

'There's someone waving at you. Look, over there by the Priory wall. It's your friend.'

Danny had started to walk over to them. He was smiling and then he recognised Adam.

'What are you doing with him? And what've you been up to?

'Another brush wi' Edmund Tarrant,' Will said.

Adam blushed. 'I'm trying to make friends. I don't want anything to do with Edmund Tarrant anymore.'

'I've remembered where I've seen you. I've seen you in the Priory.' Danny looked Adam up and down.

'Yes. My father's Reverend Jackson,' said Adam.

'I'm goin'.'

'Shall we meet later Will?'

'Not sure.'

'What's wrong?'

Will walked off. He didn't look back as he headed past the castle and towards the High Street. He wouldn't call in the George. Not like this. What was he doing in any case trying to be friends with people like Perinne and Danny? Why would Adam want to be a friend? Will didn't notice anyone as he made his way home. He turned into the road where the little row of cottages stood. There was a horse outside his house. He made his way to the door and opened it. Inside the room a tall figure was standing next to the hearth. Meg Gibbs stood as Will stepped through the door. The man turned. It was James Clarke.

'Will, what are you doing home?'

'There were no work and then I went to Cliff House.'

'But you're covered in mud.'

Will took his hat off and made a short bow to Danny's father. 'Hello, Mr Clarke.'

Meg looked from one to the other. Will made towards the steps to the attic room. He ought to tell him about the watches. Will stopped, but before he could say anything his mother spoke.

'Mr Clarke here has some news for ye, son.'

James Clarke smiled. 'Sir Charles is most pleased with your actions yesterday Will. I've brought your wages from Saturday and there are three guineas more.'

Will's eyes opened wide, astounded.

'Tell him, Mr Clarke, tell him the other news.'

'What's that then? Is he goin' to stop Edmund beatin' me up?'

'Will!'

'Sorry, mother.'

'Is that why you're muddy, lad?'

Will nodded. 'There were some watches and a snuff box. The man who took Perinne 'ad stolen 'em. Sam, me dog, he sniffed 'em out. I were takin 'em back. Edmund 'as 'em now.'

Sam was curled up in front of the fire. His eye opened at the sound of his name.

'Well, I'll look into that. But that's not my news. Sir Charles and Perinne's parents would like to reward you, maybe arrange an apprenticeship for you.'

'What kind o' apprenticeship?'

'Well, we thought to find out from Mr Clingan's Trust what can be found for you.'

'Can I choose?'

James smiled. 'I'm sure there'll be something for you. Do you wish to go and change now?'

'Yes, Mr Clarke. Are my breeches dry, mother?'

## Chapter 23

# A hiding place discovered?

'That's not like Will,' Danny said. He watched his friend walk towards the High Street.

'He'll want to get out of those clothes I expect,' Adam replied.

'I've got to get back to school. Why don't you come to the grammar school?'

'My father wanted me to board. I go to Winchester, then later Oxford I expect.'

'Is that where Edmund goes?'

'No, he has a tutor.'

The boys walked across the grass towards the Priory.

'Are you going to be a vicar too?'

'Father wants me to be, but I want to go into the law.'

'Being a vicar must be boring.'

'Not really, it's helping people.'

'And burying them. Wouldn't want to do that, Must be lots due to the smallpox.'

'That's a strange thing to say, Danny, people need to be laid to their rest. In any case, there hasn't been a burial since little Lucy Butler last week. I heard father talking about it.'

'I'd better go, the boys are going back inside.'

'Can we be friends, Danny?'

'Maybe.' Danny made his way through the side door and into the Priory.

Will looked at the coins - six golden half guineas and a silver sixpence. He'd never had so much in his hands before. He rubbed at the edge of one of the guineas and held it up between his thumb and forefinger. The King's head was staring to one side, his long hair falling over his shoulders and there were leaves around his head. What would he do with this? He could buy some new skin breeches? It wasn't a huge amount of money, but it would take him months to earn this mending nets. He stood, but the roof was low and he had to stoop. At the foot of his bed were two drawers where he kept the few clothes he had. He opened the top one and took out a clean shirt and stockings. He then pulled the whole drawer out and pushed his arm into the empty space. He brought out a small tin, opened it and looked at the coins inside. He gave his wages to his mother. Now and then she let him keep some for himself and he would try to save a few pennies. He put the half guineas into the tin. He had a few pounds now. One idea was to buy a larger boat and fish for himself. But would he ever have enough? He put the tin back into its hiding place. Sitting back on his bed, he leaned over and reached for the box he'd found on the marshes. He looked at the writing again. Perinne had said the words meant private and thirteen and were also a man's name. It was the thirteenth box. She'd also whispered to him that she'd seen more of the boxes at Danny's uncle's house. Hidden for Sir Charles Tarrant no doubt. He put the box back into its place and got dressed. Maybe she'd have more to tell this afternoon.

Perinne had been in bed since her return to Cliff House. Her mother had sat with her most of Sunday but had now retired. Lady Elizabeth's personal maid had taken her place. But now she felt fine. When Lucy had brought breakfast she'd asked her to go and fetch her mother. She wanted to meet up with Will later, but she'd have to convince everyone that she was well enough to go out alone. She got out of the large bed and walked over to the window. The daffodils had been flattened by the winds and the trees were swaying. Sitting in the window seat she thought back to what Lucy had said yesterday. If it wasn't money the kidnappers had wanted what was it - was it all to do with the machine and the boxes? It had to be. She would ask her mother.

The latch on the door lifted and Jane Menniere stepped in. She smiled and walked over to Perinne and hugged her.

'How is my darling feeling?'

'I am fine, maman. I was thinking of going for a ride on Pierre.'

'Oh, I don't think so Perinne. Dr Quartley said you must rest.'

'But I shall go mad.'

Jane stroked her daughter's forehead. 'Let me get your brush.'

Jane fetched it from the dressing table and gently teased the tangles from Perinne's long dark hair.

'Maman, why did those men take me?'

'I'm not sure. You're back safely, so try not to think of it.'

Perinne wondered how she could mention the ransom. She didn't want to get Lucy into trouble.

'Where is Millar?'

'He's gone, but Uncle Charles says that he will put out a warrant for his arrest.'

'I saw him snooping around.'

'Did you? When was this?'

'A few days ago, Thursday, I think. Ouch!'

'Sorry, try to keep your head still.'

'Please may I go out today?'

'Maybe. If so, I will come with you. I can ride Aunt Elizabeth's horse. There, all untangled. I shall get Lucy to dress it for you.'

Perinne took a breath. 'I was hoping to meet with Will again. I can be his friend now, please maman.'

'I'm not sure, Perinne. He's a common boy. Besides you won't have much time once your new governess arrives.'

'Governess? Is Mademoiselle Gareau to come here?'

'No. Aunt Elizabeth has placed an advertisement in the newspaper. You're to have an English governess.' Jane Menniere returned the brush to the dresser.

'Why is this? Are we not to go back home?' Perinne stood, her hands outstretched, questioning. 'Maman?'

'We are unlikely to return home for some time, Perinne. Please don't ask questions. It's how it is. Now, I shall go and see if it's possible to ride together this afternoon.'

Perinne watched, shocked, as her mother left the room, closing the door behind her. She returned to the window and stared out to the Needles in the distance. 'Shall I not see my home again? What about Orion?' Tears welled in her eyes at the thought of not seeing her home or her beloved horse again. And for this, and all that had happened to her, she wept.

Something was niggling in the back of Danny's mind. Will walking off had surprised him. Maybe he didn't like the idea of Adam being their friend. But that wasn't it. Would he turn up later, he wondered? And what about Perinne? Whilst she was unhurt after her kidnap she'd had a huge shock and might not be allowed out. He'd go to the beach anyway. He arrived home in time to be greeted by the smell of newly made muffins, his favourite.

'Is that you, Danny?'

His mother's voice came from the kitchen. He saw Sarah sitting at the table playing with some wooden blocks. Grandpa was nowhere to be seen.

'Did you and Jack meet father in town?'

'Yes, mother.'

'It's exciting, our Jack going to be working for Mr Oake. Father's gone with Jack to pay the premium. It means you'll be able to board!'

Danny's heart jumped. 'Board?' he said.

'School, Danny. Sir Charles has offered to help to pay as a reward for finding Miss Perinne. School for you and an apprenticeship for that boy from the town you've made friends with.'

'I don't want to go to Winchester!' Danny said.

Hannah Clarke laughed. 'I don't think Sir Charles's generosity will stretch to Winchester. Nothing's agreed yet, Danny, and let's hope he's true to his word, but it would be good for you.'

Danny made his way up the narrow staircase to his room. 'Boarding school,' he thought. He knelt on his bed and peered out of the small window. Grandpa was in the garden digging. Danny thought about how he had to read to him because Grandpa'd never learned how to read. Danny could not only read but he was learning Latin. He could read books all about the wonders of the world, the world he longed to explore. This was a big chance but what if the other boys were all like Edmund Tarrant, rich and spoiled. He'd never fit in. He watched the chickens clucking around. If he went away to school there would be more time to learn. He could learn more about science. Maybe he'd be able to invent things like the mysterious machine that the smugglers and Sir Charles were fighting over. He flopped backwards onto his bed and looked up at the ceiling. What about his friends? What about Will who had to work? Maybe Will could have his place at the free school. The thoughts buzzed and swirled around in Danny's mind. Suddenly the clock at the foot of the stairs chimed. If he was going to meet Will and Perinne today, he needed to go.

Sam was pulling a stumpy branch out of the water when Danny arrived at Muddiford. The dog dropped it at Will's feet and began to bark. Will turned to see his friend approach. Danny waved and Sam bounded towards him.

'Any sign of Perinne?'

'No,' Will said throwing the branch back into the sea. Sam ran after it.

'What was wrong with you this morning?'

Will shrugged. 'Just thinkin' 'bout me life.'

'And?'

'Things 'ave changed since then.'

'What? Since this morning?'

'Yes. I'm bein' rewarded with an apprenticeship. Don't know what though.'

'Yes, my mother told me. I may be going to a boarding school.'

'Good luck.'

'Come on, Will. Cheer up. Let's think about this mystery.

'Look, on the cliff.' Will pointed.

Perinne was shielding her eyes from the low afternoon sun. Seeing the boys she waved and nudged Pierre who trotted down the cliff towards them. The boys walked over the sands to greet her.

'Hello, my gallant rescuers,' she laughed.

Will took hold of the pony's bridle as Perinne dismounted.

'Have you told Danny of what I saw?'

'Saw what? When?' Danny looked at one, then the other.

'I discovered where some of the boxes are hidden.' Perinne looked at Will.

'Danny. Ye remember ye said ye father was involved? Well, it's not just 'im.'

'I saw some boxes at your uncle's house,' Perinne told him.

'Uncle John?'

'They were in the room upstairs, Danny, under a cloth. Are these the six Uncle Charles has?' Perinne stroked Pierre's nose.

Danny was wide-eyed and gasped in surprise.

'I have the thirteenth box so we need to find out where the other six are,' Will cut in.

'And who it is they all belong to,' Perinne said. 'Maybe you could visit your uncle and see if he will tell you anything.'

'My aunt and uncle are involved?' Danny shook his head. He put his hands in his pockets and made a circle in the sand with his foot.

'Also, Lucy said something strange to me. That Joseph said that it was not money they wanted.'

'She said that to us too!' Will exclaimed. 'The boxes, they wanted the boxes. Perinne, ye've only just arrived. Millar would have known ye were comin'. The man who kidnapped ye were in Tarrant livery. He must have been given the job by Millar.'

'It was a servant who knocked me over. Maybe it was the same one and he was making a distraction?' Danny said.

'They're all lookin' fer the boxes. Sir Charles had the town's cellars searched lookin' for ye, Perinne. But it was to look fer the smuggler's boxes too,' Will continued.

'So where can they be?' Perinne said.

'Could be 'idden anywhere.'

'Anywhere?' Danny suddenly said.

Will looked at his friend.

'Anywhere?' Danny repeated. 'Where would you hide something like that, Will?'

'With someone I'd trust.'

'And what if you didn't trust anyone?'

'I would hide them where no one would think to look,' Perinne suggested.

'Yes!' Danny said with triumph.

'Do ye think ye know, Danny?'

'Something Adam said today. It's been on my mind but I didn't know why.'

'What is it, Danny?'

'Last week, Will, the day we met, I crossed over by the graveyard behind the Castle to the Priory. There was a new grave, a little girl's, Lucy Butler. And there was another, unmarked, next to it.'

'So,' Will said.

'Adam said today that there'd been no burials since little Lucy's.'

Perinne and Will looked at each other and then back to Danny.

'Ye think that's where the boxes could be?'

'Why not?'

'The damp, the wet, Danny, boxes rot, they'd spoil.'

'Yours was in the water and it was all right, wasn't it? Let's go and look.'

'What if they are in the grave? What is it we should do?' Perinne asked.

'There's someone watching us, look, on the cliff,' Danny whispered.

'It is my maman. She is riding with me. She said that I could come and speak with you. It means it is time for me to go.'

'What about looking at the grave?'

'How would I get to Christchurch at night to help?' Perinne said, frustration etched on her face.

'Who'd want to go to the graveyard at night, with all the ghosts walking?'

'More smugglers' tales, Danny,' Will laughed. 'I'll go and check tonight. I'll take Sam. Meet 'ere again tomorrow. If they're there we'll make plans to get 'em out.'

## Chapter 24

# Smugglers gather

Will made his way home with Sam at his heels. The mystery was nearer to being solved, but what would they do with the boxes if they were in the grave? These men were dangerous. Maybe they should tell Sir Charles and let him deal with it. He looked up at the dull sky warmed by a sun struggling to shine through. Seagulls, sparkling white against the dark clouds, squawked. Should he look now or wait? He would need a lamp or a flame if he came at night. Dusk would be best. He'd be able to see what he was doing, but it should be dark enough not to be noticed. But how would he know where to look? He decided he'd go to the Quay, cutting behind the Castle, the same as Danny had done a week ago. He reached the town bridge and could see folk ahead clearing away after the market. Hopefully few people would be near the graveyard now. He went through the gate with Sam running on ahead. Gravestones loomed, casting eerie shadows along the quivering grass. Will looked around as he walked. Had Danny simply passed through or should he walk amongst the graves? Ahead, Sam had stopped and was sniffing around the ground. He started to scratch at something.

'Sam, stop that!' Will shouted.

As Will ran towards the dog a new gravestone caught his eye, and next to the grave was disturbed ground.

He'd found exactly what he was looking for. Getting his bearings, he'd return in an hour.

Isaac had stayed off the ale for a whole day. Market day or not, he'd heard Meekwick Ginn was in town. Rumours were about that Ginn had something to do with the kidnapping of the girl from Cliff House. John Hewitt had told him young Will had got himself involved and was some kind of hero. There'd been a visit from one of Sir Charles Tarrant's men to see Meg Gibbs today, he'd seen him arrive. Also there'd been whisperings of 'a movement of goods' in the next few days and he'd promised John he'd find out as much as he could. He made his way first to the George. It was bustling, Monday night was always busy. Reek's wagon had just returned from Poole and the post was being gathered for the post-chaise which left later. Isaac recognised some of the market traders sipping ale bought with some of the spoils of their day. Beth Gibbs, with her beautiful smile, was weaving around carrying trays of ale. But he couldn't see who he was looking for. He turned and left for the Eight Bells.

Edmund dug the spurs of his boots into his horse's haunches and galloped away from Cliff House. He was furious. Not only had that awful girl told his father that the scab town boy had found the watches, but worse, she was going to be staying at Cliff House for the near future. Simon followed behind, struggling to keep up. There was just enough light to see the road but soon they reached the town. The lamplighter had yet to start his rounds. Edmund thought of the link-boys he'd seen in Bath leading gentry with their cotton-tow lanterns. That'd be a job for the Gibbs boy - a farthing a time. Why was his father wasting money on him? As Edmund thought about Will he swore he caught sight of him at the top of the road. When he looked again the boy had gone.

'What will we do here, Edmund?'

Simon rode his horse alongside his friend.

'Look.'

'For what?'

'When father sent out the Dragoons to look for the French girl he asked them to look for something else.'

'What?'

'I don't know.'

'Then what's the point? Let's go back. Let's go to the Ship in Distress. We can get ale there.'

'We can get some here.'

'Edmund, this is a waste of time.'

'The Eight Bells, we'll go there.'

Edmund nudged his horse and they trotted along the road. Straw from the pens of the Monday market whispered around their hooves. Turning into Church Street they dismounted.

As Isaac approached the old ale house, two well-dressed youths were handing their horses to the stable boy. One he recognised as Edmund Tarrant but he didn't know the other boy. He went inside. He noticed Caleb Brown, the bearded blacksmith, clutching his pipe with his huge grimy hands, listening to another man whose face Isaac couldn't see. Caleb nodded at Isaac. Across the room he smiled to himself as he noticed Ginn sitting in the corner with Guy Cox, a tanned-skinned fisherman. He bought a tankard of ale and moved over to stand by the fireside, hoping to listen in on as much of the conversation as he could.

Edmund pressed a farthing into the stable boy's hand and stepped into the alehouse with Simon following behind him. The stone floor was littered with dirty straw and the air hung with a day-full of smoke. Candles were already lit, the smell of tallow mixing with the sweat of working men. Edmund peered around to see a familiar face sitting in a corner deep in conversation. As he approached Meekwick Ginn he was unaware of Isaac watching him.

Will crept around the wall into the narrow pathway beside the last house before the Priory gates. He made his way along, feeling the wall's rough bricks. The sun had set but dusk glowed dark blue across the grass. The honey-coloured gravestones were now shadowy blocks. An owl hooted. He was soon at the new grave of the little girl. He knelt on the dewy grass and felt around where he'd seen the marks of newly cut sods. His fingers caught the edge and he pushed them down easily into the damp soil. The sod was only an inch or two thick. He glanced around then pulled at the grass, lifting a length back a few inches, revealing a piece of wooden plank. The plank was wedged into the earth but there was a small gap. Will could see nothing in the dark below. He took off his coat and laid it on the grass, then rolled his sleeve up and lay down on his stomach. He could feel the cold biting through the thin cotton of his shirt. He pushed his arm through the gap and felt around. Nothing. 'There 'as to be something 'ere,' he thought. He inched nearer the edge of the grave and reached again. This time, as his hand touched wood, his heart started to pound. What if it was just a new grave, what if Danny was wrong, or maybe Adam had misheard his father? A sudden burst of laughter from the back of the nearby houses reminded him of how near he was to people. He'd be in deep trouble if he were caught interfering with graves. He sat up. What should he do? He pushed the grass back further and saw the plank was wedged on a small ledge. He tugged at it. Earth trickled down the side of the grave, pattering onto the wood below. He wished he had a lamp. His eyes though were getting used to the darkness. He lay down again. He could see the faint outline of one long box. On top of this were five other boxes, three were small ones, similar to the one he had at home. The other two were much bigger. He quickly replaced the plank and the grass. Brushing dirt from his sleeve he picked up his coat and shook it. He then trod around the grass to push it back in place. Hopefully no one would notice it had been disturbed.

Isaac watched as Meekwick Ginn sipped his brandy and spoke. He strained to hear what Ginn was saying.

'Millar's gone, the fool, Tarrant's put a warrant out.'

Guy Cox leaned forward. 'What about Litty an' Pike?'

'Pike's none the worse for his beatin' by the boys. He couldn't have expected that, clever as he is. He and Litty are making the arrangements to move the stuff tomorrow night. Tarrant's getting close and ...'

'What is it?'

Isaac turned too. So they were moving the goods. But he still didn't know where from. He'd stay for a little while longer.

'Shh,' Ginn whispered. 'That's Tarrant's son.'

'Does he know you?'

'He's coming over. Not a word about this business.'

Isaac inched a little closer. He now knew things were moving. Maybe young Tarrant would give away some more information.

Edmund held out his hand, but Ginn didn't take it.

'Mr Ginn, isn't it?'

'And what's it to you?'

'You're a friend of my father.'

'So? What do you want?'

'Were you disappointed the shoot was cancelled?'

'Look, boy, I'm not interested. Leave us in peace.'

Edmund wasn't going to give in that easily. 'And you're a friend of Millar - my father's put a price on his head.'

Ginn took a deep breath. 'Millar's no friend of mine.'

'Then it's a strange thing you talking to him, bringing in that coach not long after the kidnapping.'

Ginn moved uncomfortably in his seat. 'Look, what is your name, I forget.'

'And you had time to leave the ransom note,' Edmund said, sneering.

'Leave Mr Ginn alone,' said Guy.

'Who are you? Don't you know who my father is?'

'I said leave us be.' Guy stood and made to get a hold of Edmund.

'Calm down,' Ginn growled.

'Don't you dare strike me! My father'd see you hung!'

The room had gone quiet and all eyes were on the pair. Caleb Brown stood and moved over towards them. He towered above both Edmund and Guy. He didn't speak but glared at them. Simon looked at Edmund, terrified.

'Come on, Edmund, let's go.'

'Sit down.' Ginn pointed at a stool beside the table. 'Hold your tongue, I don't think your father would take kindly to his business being shouted around an alehouse.'

Edmund sat down. Simon stayed in the shadows. Caleb returned to his seat. Isaac turned his back, not wanting to be seen staring. The murmurs of conversation started again.

'Yes, I know your father. I hear the girl's back safely.'

'Yes.'

'You don't seem too pleased about it.' Ginn squinted, his ghostly face mottled in the candlelight.

Edmund scoffed. 'Father wasn't that concerned, he used it as an excuse.'

'Excuse for what?'

It was Edmund's turn to shift on his seat. He decided to take a chance. 'I thought maybe you'd know what, seeing as he's a friend. Then I could help father find whatever he's looking for. He might reward me and not riff raff. In any case, those kidnappers missed an opportunity. The French girl and her scabby friends know something. Maybe that's why they kidnapped her, and not for any ransom.'

Ginn leaned forward in the seat. 'I can't help you there, lad,' he lied. 'I don't know anything. But if you hear of any way I can help your father, you let me know.'

Isaac supped the last dregs of his ale and turned to leave. There was no more information coming from Ginn tonight. But tomorrow night was another matter. He had to get a message to John Hooper and speak to Will Gibbs.

Will made his way back down Church Street. Lamps were now lit and he'd soon be home for something to eat. It had been a long day, so he had to look twice when he saw Edmund sitting in the Eight Bells with Guy Cox and the man with the pale face.

## Chapter 25

# Shall we tell?

Perinne hated the idea of Danny and Will finding the other boxes without her. Maybe they weren't hidden in the graveyard. If they were they'd have to get them after dark. How could she get there? She knew her way to town now and could ride Pierre there, but the stable boy would know. She was still being watched after her capture. Were the ghosts real? And where would they hide the boxes if they found them? Then there was the problem of who the boxes belonged to. Last week she'd overheard Uncle Charles saying it was her parents who'd told him about the machine and that it was coming to England to be sold. He'd had men lay in wait for its arrival. But he'd said it had been stolen, so whose machine was it? Maybe she should just tell her father what they knew.

The door opened, it was Lucy with the breakfast tray.

'You are late this morning, Lucy.'

'Sorry, miss.' Lucy's eyes moistened and a tear trickled down her cheek.

'What is wrong?'

Lucy bit her lips.

'Lucy?'

'My father. He's had an accident. One o' the horses bolted in the stable last night. His leg's hurt and it's the one's that's bad already. Sir Charles is angry, what with

Millar goin'. It only leaves the stable boy.' Lucy began to sob. Perinne took her maid's hand.

'Come on, Lucy. I am sure that he will soon be well again.'

'But it might take some time, miss. We'll 'ave to go to the parish.'

'The parish? I do not know what you mean.'

'For poor relief, miss. There'll only be my wages to feed six of us, and buy medicine. I only earn a shillin' an' a few pence a week.'

'Oh, Lucy. I shall ask maman if there is something that can be done to help.'

After breakfast Perinne went to the drawing room to find her mother or father. Her father, she was told, was with Uncle Charles in the library. Her mother was not yet downstairs, but Aunt Elizabeth was sitting by the window, needlework in hand.

'Perrine, dear, have you come to do some stitching?'

'I am looking for maman,' Aunt Elizabeth.

'I'm sure your mother will be here soon. Now, tell me, are you fully recovered? I hear you went riding yesterday.'

'I am fine, aunt. I shall go riding again this afternoon.'

'Well, I'm pleased to hear it. The sea air will do you good.'

'Aunt?'

'Yes, dear.'

'Are we able to help Lucy and her family? She is most upset.'

'I'm sure that Susan can send some food and I shall see to it. Uncle Charles has already thought about the horses. He's advertising in the *Journal* for someone to replace that wicked Millar. He's also going to ask the boy in town who rescued you. He made a good job of helping on Saturday night and we know he's of good character. He could learn to do Scott's job until he's well.'

Perinne tried hard not to show emotion. 'Will – here?' she thought.

'That will be good,' she said. 'He is a nice boy, but what of his job?'

'Oh, I shan't get involved with all that. I prefer to leave such worries to the men folk.'

The *Solomon* left Christchurch Harbour early in the morning on the first high tide of the day. Will was disappointed that there was no work for him again. But the day was to be a fair one, with mild winds and sunshine. He needed to think. He watched as Guy Cox raised the ochre-coloured sail. It wouldn't surprise Will if he were involved in taking the boxes. Guy had persuaded Master Hardyman to haul in sunken barrels before now, each attached by cord to bottle corks which marked the spot where they'd been left in the sea. Guy may be a smuggler, but was he a kidnapper? He wasn't the man in the coach. Will would've recognised him, even with a mask. He could have been the driver out on the seat with Millar. Maybe it had been Guy who Danny had seen on his way to get Tom Pike from gaol. The salty air blew at Will's face as he thought what to do. He also needed to think about tonight. Could they really get the boxes and, if they did, where could they put them?

'Will.'

Will turned, it was James Clarke.

'No work again, boy?'

'Nay, Mr Clarke. Nor any nets fer stitchin'.'

'Well, there's some work for you at Cliff House, if you're interested.'

Will's spirits picked up, until Edmund came into mind. James read his thoughts.

'Master Edmund's been instructed to leave you be.'

'What work is it then?' Will asked.

'Helping in the stables, and footman's work. Can you ride?'

'A little - not 'ad much chance.'

'Well, it's more mucking out, grooming and cleaning saddles. Are you interested?'

'Aye, Mr Clarke, I'll give it a try.'

'They're movin the stuff t'night,' said Isaac.

Isaac had set out for Hinton at noon. He'd missed Will who'd left early to get work on the boat. He'd try to speak with him later.

'Did you get word out to our gang?' Uncle John answered.

'Aye, told 'em we need to act quickly too if we're to catch Ginn and his gang moving the goods,' said Isaac, who was now sitting in the window seat.

Uncle John paced up and down the small room. 'Aye, I'll get the trap ready. We'll call in at Burton first.'

Danny looked out to sea. Cormorants, having finished hunting for food, had settled on the sandbank and were holding their black, cape-like wings out to dry. The fishermen would try to kill them, saying they took too many fish. Uncle John said he'd heard stories of Chinese people using them to catch fish. As he watched the boats on the glistening bay he wondered if Will had come across anything in the graveyard. There was no sign of him yet. The boats had gone out early, so he should be back by now. Suddenly someone whistled. Danny turned, he couldn't see anyone.

'Danny.' The shout seemed to come from a distance. Then he saw two figures on horseback on the cliff top, the sun lighting up their faces. It was Perinne and with her it looked like Will. It couldn't be. The two figures waved, then restarted their ride. As they got closer Danny was astonished to see it was Will.

'What's going on?' Danny asked as his friends reached the beach.

'My new footman,' Perinne laughed. 'Poor Lucy. Her father is hurt and we needed help.'

'Is this your new apprenticeship then, Will?'

'Don't think so, but 'tis work. And before you ask, Edmund isn't to come near me.'

'I expect he doesn't like that very much.'

'Tell Danny your other news, Will,' Perinne said.

Will jumped off his horse and patted its neck. He held the reins. 'There's boxes in the grave. Six as I counted. One of 'em's a big'n.'

'So, what shall we do?' Danny asked.

'I should tell my papa,' Perinne said. She was still on her pony.

'Is something wrong?' Danny said.

Will looked at Perinne.

'Perinne thinks we should just let 'er father know. Leave 'em to it. Come on, Danny, think about it. Those smugglers are bad folk, don't forget they've pistols and ... well ...'

'What is it? Tell me.' Danny looked anxiously at his friend.

'It's ... just ...,' Will closed his eyes, trying hard to fight back the tears. He took a deep breath. 'It's how me father died.' Will turned and pressed his head gently against the horse's neck. Perinne slid from her saddle, took Will's hand and gave it a sympathetic squeeze.

'Your father was a smuggler?' Danny was aghast.

'I've told ye. Most people round these parts are involved some way.'

'How did it happen?'

'Three year ago now. He were wi' a large gang o' men. Just along 'ere.' Will pointed along the beach. 'It were a big cargo. There were twenty or thirty men bringin' three or four boatloads onto the beach. Wagons were waitin' to take the goods far and wide. It were a wild night by all accounts, wind lashing, high waves crashing onto the beach. It were well planned and would've passed well, save for some snitch tellin' the Revenue.'

Danny didn't know what to say.

'Father were shot in the leg. They fetched 'im 'ome. Paid the surgeon in brandy to come an' see 'im. But it got infected. Mother tried her 'erbs but father became ill, and died.'

The three stood motionless. All that could be heard was the rhythmic ebb and flow of the waves.

Will broke the silence. 'I were just ten. Made me promise to father I'd watch after mother an' me sister. I've tried to keep from trouble. Wouldn't do for me to go out an' get shot too.'

'It is the same with Lucy, her father has hurt his leg also. I hope that he will be all right,' Perrine said.

'I'm sorry, Will,' Danny said. 'I can't imagine what it's like not having my father around. What shall we do? Shall we tell Sir Charles about the grave?'

Will walked over to the water's edge. Danny and Perinne

looked at each other. Will picked up a stone and skimmed it across the water. He suddenly seemed distant, deep in his thoughts. After several minutes of silence he turned to his friends.

'No. We wanted an adventure,' he called over.

'What then?' Danny asked.

Will walked back. 'We'll get the boxes at dusk. We'll 'ide 'em nearby. The smugglers won't go 'til after dark.'

'Hide them where?'

'Not the Castle, the hill's too steep, but we could use the fallen stones to cover 'em.'

'Perhaps Adam Jackson can help.'

'We don't know 'im. Adam could change 'is mind about being Edmund's friend.'

'What about me? I can help,' Perinne said.

'Ye won't be able to get away, Perinne,' Will answered.

'I will find a way to be there.' Perinne climbed onto Pierre.

'It's dangerous, Perinne, not for girls,' cut in Danny. 'They didn't hurt you last time but if they caught you again, who knows?'

'I want to be there and I shall find a way!' Perinne nudged the pony and trotted away towards the cliff.

'I 'ave to get after 'er,' Will said. 'Meet me by the castle at six.' Will mounted his horse and rode after Perinne.

'What time are you to meet Sir George?' Sir Charles asked James Clarke.

'Seven, sir.'

'And you're sure the goods are being moved tonight?'

'Yes, I've a gang in town. We've yet to find out exactly where the goods are hidden. We will though. The men are instructed to watch out, then ambush them and seize the spoils. It could get nasty. It seems Tom Pike's involved after all.'

'Oh?'

'Danny said the kidnapper's face had pox marks - the man he described has to be Pike. It's possible his escape was planned for this job. But as the goods were brought in earlier than expected, he missed the chance to lead the gang. Sir, Pike's reputation for organising the smuggling gangs is well known in these parts, as is his reputation for avoiding being caught. I expect Ginn secured his services for this plot.'

'Ginn. I can't believe he's the paymaster.' Sir Charles banged his fist on his desk. 'It all fits into place, him recommending Millar too. But to tonight's work.'

Yves Menniere spoke. 'I will ride in with James also. We need many men in town tonight. But *you* must stay away, Charles.'

'I agree,' James Clarke said.

'You're right, it wouldn't do for me to be seen around if there's fighting. But I'll see Pike goes to the gallows this time!'

## Chapter 26

# Ghosts in the graveyard

Danny wondered how Will could get to the castle on time. It was gone four now. Will had to get back to Cliff House with Perinne and then walk all the way home. Danny needed to get home himself. What would he do if he weren't allowed out after supper? As he crossed Purewell for the Burton road, he thought he could see Uncle John in the trap heading towards the town. There was another man with him. Perhaps it was just someone who looked like him.

Isaac and Uncle John arrived at Isaac's cottage near the Bargate. Inside smelled damp. The place was gloomy and what little furniture dusty.

'You need a woman about the house, Isaac.'

'Pah. I've tried to win over Meg Gibbs but she'll 'ave none of it. We'll call around there, see what we can find out. Tarrant's lad told Ginn young Will knows something. He knew enough to find out from me where Millar lived.'

'Aye, he heard the fight on the marsh too,' said John. 'Now, let's look at tonight. There's five o' us so far. You, me, Caleb Brown, Moses Pilgrim and David Preston.'

'What about Henry Lane?' Isaac asked.

'He's in with Guy Cox, so chances are he'll be with him tonight. John Brown as well.'

Isaac shook his head. 'I don't like it, John. These are our friends an' neighbours, an' what will we get for it - a few guineas? While the venturers get richer. What's in these boxes anyway?'

'Not sure. James says somethin' of importance but hasn't said what it is.'

'Haven't ye had a look?'

'Tried but can't see how to get in 'em. Didn't want to force one open - it'd show.'

'An' how many are we expectin' to find?'

'Seven. There's thirteen altogether an' I have six back home. They'll be different sizes and the thirteenth is amongst 'em and this is the one we must have, according to James.'

Isaac looked out of the small window. 'Well, I've some bread, a bite of meat an' some ale. We'll have that an' watch out for Will.'

'I've told the men to meet by the Quomps at eleven. If we don't see him before then, he'll have to keep his secrets.'

'Perinne! Wait!'

Will rode gingerly, not used to being on a horse. He could've run quicker. Pierre slowed and Perinne looked back at Will.

'See, you say that danger is not for girls but you are afraid to ride a horse fast.'

'It wasn't me that said it.'

'You need me tonight.'

'All I said was that ye'd have trouble gettin' away.'

'And so may you. What if you have more duties on our return?'

Perinne is right, thought Will. When they returned to Cliff House his luck was in, Joseph was waiting.

'Ye can get off home now, lad. Tell ye mother ye'll be livin' here for a week and that ye can go home next Monday.'

Will led the horses into the stable where Ben, the stable boy, took them from him.

'I shall see you and Danny by the castle at six, and beware of the phantoms,' Perinne said and walked away before Will could reply.

Just over an hour later, and unaware that she was being watched by Edmund, Perinne left the stables and rode Pierre down the driveway. She'd told Ben that should anyone ask, she was taking some food to Lucy's family and to find out how John Scott was. There'd be enough light to get to town and she was sure she'd find her way back again. Hopefully the moon would be up by the time they'd finished their night's work.

The ruined castle stood high on its hill in shades of grey against the darkening sky. Few people were about. Danny pulled his scarf snugly around his neck and left the road. His father hadn't been at home and he'd told his mother he was going to see his friend. It wasn't a lie really. Jack had also asked him where he was going. He was going to see his friend Tom and they could walk together, but Danny had made an excuse. Now he was wondering which direction Will would come from. He crept carefully around the back of the castle. He didn't usually believe in ghosts, and then occasionally he wondered if they were real. Boys in school sometimes said they'd seen the spirits of monks walking above the Priory nave and in the grounds. The bottom of the hill was scattered with loose stones. Danny looked around for a possible hiding place for the boxes. The old house would be too obvious. He thought about making his way towards the grave. Then he saw Will. He was on the water. Danny smiled. He hadn't thought about moving the boxes on the river. But how would they get across the mill stream without using the bridge?

Will climbed out of the boat followed by Sam. Danny was surprised he had the dog with him. Will dragged the little boat onto the bank and over the grass. Then he launched it into the mill stream, climbed in and pushed it the few feet across the water. As he watched Will tie the boat to a tree by the old ruined house, Danny thought back to Will's confession that his father was a smuggler. He remembered too what Will had said about catching rabbits. He was probably a poacher too. If his father found out he'd not be allowed to see Will again, despite their recent courage. Will soon reached the castle. Danny patted Sam who ran off to sniff around.

'We'll wait a while. Let it get darker,' Will said. 'We need to plan 'ow we'll move the boxes an' where to 'ide 'em.'

The boys sat in the chill of the castle's shadow. The sails of a boat on the river were being lowered. The quiet that had begun to settle in the town was now an eerie stillness. The gulls had roosted and the echo of distant chattering voices was the only sound. Lamplight flickered from Dr Quartley's house, casting a shallow glow into the road. Then a pony appeared trotting along.

'Look, Will,' Danny whispered, pointing. 'I don't believe it.'

Will shook his head. 'I do.'

The little Forester left the road and made towards the castle. Its rider was dark, like a spectre. Perinne was covered from head to foot, completely wrapped up in her cape with her face only just visible.

'How did you get away?' said Danny.

'It was easy, and I shall return so. No one will know that I have been out.'

'Will's come on his boat, it's over there. That's where we'll put the boxes.'

'I have brought some sacks,' Perinne said.

'And I have rope. Come on, let's go now before anyone see us,' Will added.

Danny and Will led and Perinne followed, Pierre clipping his hooves on the stones. They were quickly at the graveside.

Soon Will had lifted the grass from the top of the plank. Danny took one end and between them they lifted the wood clear and laid it to one side. Perinne had got down from the pony and was standing at the side looking into the dark hole. Will and Danny knelt down. Will bent into the hollow and began to lift the boxes, handing them to Danny. The three small boxes came first. Danny passed them on to Perinne one by one. She could make out letters. They were the same as those on the box at Hinton. *Dix, Onze, Huit*. She put them into the sack and took them to the boat. Danny had to help to lift the next box. It was four times the size of the smaller ones and heavier. *Cinq*. They set it beside the grave and reached down for the next. *Sept*. Perinne arrived back and bent to lift one of the waiting boxes.

'Be careful, it's 'eavy,' Will whispered. 'Let Danny take that, you 'elp me lift this one.'

Perinne swapped places and Danny took the box away.

'Ye'll be in trouble if ye're found out,' Will said.

'What can they do? Nothing, I am here now.'

'Woof!'

'Shhh, Sam, it's Danny coming back.'

Danny was running. 'I've just seen Edmund.'

'Did he see ye?'

'No, he was with Simon. Come on, let's get the job done.'

'We've a problem,' said Will. 'This last box is much too 'eavy, we'll never lift it.'

The final box took up the whole length and width of the grave and was chained.

'Rrrrr, woof!'

'Sam!'

Perinne gasped. 'Look!'

Someone was coming towards them holding a lamp.

'Who's there? Stop what you're doing. You'll be whipped for meddling with graves!'

The figure lifted the lamp, illuminating the face of its owner.

'Adam!' Danny said, in a hushed voice.

'You. Oh, it's the three of you! What are you doing?'

'It's not what you think,' Danny answered.

'We have to get these boxes out,' said Perinne, 'they are stolen. We need to get them to the people to whom they belong.'

Adam looked at the box at the side of the grave.

'This one's too 'eavy,' Will said, pointing into the hole. 'Can ye 'elp us lift it out?'

'Then what?' Danny said. 'Your boat will sink with that one in it.'

'Then bring it into the Priory, we'll hide it there,' offered Adam.

Adam and Danny knelt at one end, Will and Perinne were at the other. Adam had set down his lamp at the edge, its flickering light catching on the brown chain. They stretched down and took hold of the chain.

'Ready? Pull!' Will ordered.

The four groaned with the weight of the box.

'It's too heavy,' Danny sighed.

'Pierre,' Perinne said. 'He can pull this for us, if we pull it to the edge.'

'Come on, everyone to this end,' Adam said, joining in eagerly.

The four heaved at the chain. The end of the box rose, making a clattering noise from inside. They rested the end on the edge of the grass. Will got up and went to get Pierre who had been tethered to a nearby tree. He lifted the coil of rope that he'd earlier hung in a loop from the saddle. Using the rope, he attached one end to Pierre's saddle, and tied the other end to the chain around the box. Then the little pony began to pull.

'Wait!' Danny shouted. 'It'll leave tracks. People will follow them.'

'Then open the box and we'll carry the things into the Priory piece by piece,' Adam suggested. 'But I can't see how it opens.'

'And we need to get the chain off,' Danny added.

'The chain's an easy job, look, it's just a clasp catchin' it,' Will said. 'An' I think I know 'ow to open it. If it's the same as the one I 'ave.'

'You have a box?' asked Adam.

'Not as big as this one,' Will smiled as he unhooked the chain.

Danny and Adam took hold of one end and Will and Perinne the other. Holding the box as Will instructed them they pulled. The box slid apart. Inside were long rolls of metal, several rods, coiled chains and large cogs. One by one they took them across the graveyard to a small door and into the Priory.

'Hide them here,' Adam said. 'No one will look here.'

Finally they brought the last of the parts and the box itself.

'I'll find something to cover it. You be gone and finish your task.' At that, Adam took his lamp and disappeared into the darkness of the ancient building.

Will, Danny and Perinne replaced the plank and stamped down the grass over the grave. Will lifted the last box to take with him to the boat. Soon they were back at the foot of the castle.

'I'll go on 'ome now. I'll leave the boxes in the boat. I'll cover 'em up, no one will touch 'em. I'll be at Cliff House from now, Danny. Can ye get over there tomorrow?'

'I'll try.'

Will walked off and Danny and Perinne watched as Sam jumped into the boat followed by Will and the pair rowed away. Danny made a cradle with his hands and helped Perinne into her saddle. He walked alongside her as they left for the road.

'See,' she said, 'I told you all would be well.'

'Danny!'

'Perinne!'

The two looked in shock as James Clarke and Yves Menniere rode across the bridge towards them.

## Chapter 27

# The last straw

Will pushed away from the bank and rowed north along the stream. Luckily the rain of recent days had made the water higher than usual. The boxes weren't too heavy. At the low bridge, he had to lie flat to go beneath, pushing with his hands under the mossy arch. Occasionally the bottom of the boat caught the little stream's bed, but he soon reached the river. The moon had risen, sending a streak of silver light across the surface. The water lapped the bank as he pulled the oars to steer himself around the river bend and to home. He was exhausted after his early start and the events of the day. His eyelids, heavy, closed. The splash of a fish leaping in the water jolted him awake. He reached the bank and tied the boat in its usual place and covered the boxes with the spare sacks. Sam jumped out of the boat and ran on ahead of his master.

'Grrrr ...'

'What is it?'

'Grrrr ...'

'Sam?'

Suddenly, out of the shadows two horses appeared.

'You're home then, ruffian?' Edmund scoffed. 'It stinks around here.'

Will's heart sank. He wasn't in the mood for Edmund again. 'Ye've been told to keep away from me. Go away,' he said wearily.

'I've to keep away from you at Cliff House, not in town.'

'What do ye want, Edmund?'

'Master Edmund to you, I'm sick of you, town boy. You think you've found favour with my father, playing the hero. But all he's done is made you a fart follower. Well, I'm going to see to it you never come to Cliff House again.' Edmund jumped down from his horse and drew a dagger. Sam started to bark. Will bent down and picked up a thick branch lying by the track.

Edmund laughed and lunged at Will who lifted the branch and struck back. Sam snarled and pounced to bite, but Edmund kicked at the dog, catching its haunches. Sam yelped.

'Come on, Simon, help me,' Edmund shouted. Simon stared. 'Come on,' Edmund demanded.

'Get away from me 'ome, get back to yer big 'ouse and fancy things,' Will shouted.

Edmund lunged again, the dagger point catching Will on the face and Will struck him hard on the shoulder.

'What's goin' on?'

The shout came from behind Simon. Two figures approached. It was Isaac. Will was surprised to see Danny's Uncle John following him.

'Get away, go on. Ye bloods aren't welcome round 'ere, away wi' ye.' Isaac yelled. He was waving an old pan. 'Leave the lad be, he's better than ten o' ye despite ye breedin'.'

'Will!' A scream pierced the cold air. Meg Gibbs came running out of the cottage and over to Edmund. She began to thump him.

Edmund, distracted, was trying to push her away when Isaac swiped at him with the pan, catching him hard across the back of his head and knocking off his hat. Edmund yowled in pain. By now other neighbours had appeared, they cheered as Edmund took the blow. Furious he plunged his dagger in its sheath then bent to grab his hat from the floor. A pain shot though his shoulder where Will had hit it. Then Isaac wielded the pan to take another swing. Edmund managed to duck out of the way. Rubbing his head, he mounted his horse, kicked its haunches and rode off with Simon cowering behind him.

'This won't be the last you hear of me, lout!' Edmund bawled.

Will stood, shocked. He felt a warm trickle, falling down his cheek like a tear. He wiped it with the back of his hand.

'Come on home, Will,' his mother said. 'We need to clean yer face.' She was crying.

'Thank ye Isaac, John.' Meg nodded to the two who were standing watching Edmund disappear from the end of the track.

Neighbours scurried, muttering, back into their little cottages.

Will went into their tiny home and sat down at the table. Sam settled in front of what little fire burned in the grate. He began licking his side.

'Oh, Will, whatever's happening fer the young gentleman to come along here to attack you?' Meg said, as she started to dab at the cut. Then she wiped another tear with the back of her sleeve and sniffed.

'Gentleman?' Will mocked. 'Beggar folk have better ways than Edmund Tarrant.'

'Don't go a gettin' yerself in trouble with Sir Charles, he can see ye hung!'

'He were offerin' me an apprenticeship a couple o' days ago, Mother, an' it were his son as started it. He were waitin' for me, folks can confirm it.'

Meg finished wiping Will's cut. 'I'm sorry, son. I have to go. I'm off to the George to help Beth. Mr Martin's on some business tonight, sounded important, an' I can't turn down the money, will ye be all right alone?'

'I don't think they'll be back, mother, not tonight.'

Meg put on her bonnet and dragged a shawl around her shoulders. 'Well, I'll be gone then. But go to Isaac if there's any more trouble.' At that Meg left.

Will tried to put Edmund from his thoughts. At least he hadn't known about the boxes and that they were just feet away. Perinne would know what the words on the boxes were, more numbers probably and they'd prove they were the ones everyone wanted. He took a ladle of broth from the pot over the fire and sipped it. 'Who did they belong to?' he thought. And worse, was he in more danger now he had them in his boat? Not unless anyone found out. And what about the one he had hidden by his bed? A knock on the door startled him.

'Will, Will lad, answer the door.'

Will was surprised Isaac hadn't followed his mother. Wearily he got up and lifted the latch.

'We need to speak wi ye, lad.'

Will looked out at his old neighbour and at Danny's Uncle John who was standing behind him.

'Thank you, Isaac, Mr Hewitt. It were a good thing ye both came when ye did.'

'Ye were puttin' up a good fight, lad.

'What is it? Mother's left.'

'She's a great woman beating young Tarrant like that, but it's you we want words with.' Isaac moved to step in but Will stood firm. 'Come on, lad, let us in.'

Will pulled the door open. 'I'm ready fer me bed. Isaac, but seein' as ye've saved me life t'night.'

The two old men stepped through the door.

'It's like this, Will,' Isaac began. 'Word 'as it ye know about a load as come in last week.'

'Oh no,' Will thought, then he had an idea.

'I've not been on the boat for days now, there's been no work for me.'

'Nah. Not goods coming off the *Solomon*, somethin' else.'

Will started to feel uneasy. What should he say? They had to be working for Sir Charles, but he'd seen Isaac with Ginn. But they'd just rescued him from a beating, or worse, so he took a deep breath.

'Don't know 'bout any load,' he said.

'Well I've heard tell it isn't so. Like father like son, eh?'

'I've 'ad nothin' to do wi' smugglin', Isaac. I promised father I'd take care o' mother. Can't do that if I get meself killed or lost at sea, can I?'

'Ye've got yerself friendly wi' me nephew, Will. Ye've both been up to somethin', and the French girl,' Uncle John said.

'We're just friends, nothin' more.' Will's heart was thumping. What did they know? Had they been seen in the graveyard?

'We've heard diff'rent,' Isaac butted in. Uncle John stepped forward.

'Look, Will, ye're a good lad. If ye hear anything let us know. There are some bad people out there after some goods as don't belong to 'em. Ye could be in danger. If ye know anythin' I suggest ye let Danny's father know. Come on, Isaac, let's go.'

The two men left and Will closed the door. He was shaking. What should he do? He snuffed out the candle and went up the step ladder to bed, though he didn't sleep much.

Danny and Perinne had been put into one of the bedrooms at the George. Will's sister Beth had brought them each a glass of small beer. They seemed to have been waiting hours.

'I wonder who is staying in this room,' Perinne said.

'Who cares,' Danny replied. 'We're in deep trouble this time.'

The door opened. It was James and Yves.

'Now,' said James, 'I want an explanation. No tales, just the truth.'

As Danny and Perinne looked at each other a long-faced man with greying brown hair entered the room – Sir George Cook.

'So, you two young ones, why are you out and about in town so late? A courtin'?' The man said.

'No, certainly not,' Perinne insisted.

Danny laughed. 'No sir, we were ...,' he hesitated and looked at Perinne.

'We have been solving a mystery,' Perinne said.

'Really, and what is it? Is it solved?'

'Almost.'

'Then what will bring this mystery to an end?'

James Clarke and Yves Menniere looked at each other, intrigued.

'Well, *ma petite*?' Yves asked.

'I think that Uncle Charles has been looking for some boxes. We know where they are.'

'Oh, and where are they?' asked Sir George, cupping his chin in the hook of his thumb and forefinger.

'Ah, this is our problem,' Perinne continued. 'We do not yet know to whom the boxes belong, so how can we return them?'

'They belong to no one, Perinne. They were stolen and maman and I found out they were coming to England. We told your uncle,' her father said.

'But if they were stolen, then they do not belong to Uncle Charles.'

'I cannot explain at the moment, *ma petite*, but please

tell us. Sir George is going to make sure these boxes get to the right people.'

'Who are the right people?' Danny cut in.

'I belong to the Royal Society,' the man said. 'For over one hundred years members of the Society have met to talk about science and watch wondrous experiments. Danny, your father wrote to me for Sir Charles. The boxes contain parts of a machine. The inventor is dead, but I know someone in America who may be able to put the machine together. If this machine can be made then it will change the world.'

John and Isaac drove in the trap to the edge of Creedy's Field. From here they could watch for the others arriving near to the Quomps, marshland by the water's edge, which was too boggy to walk across. They'd have to be careful not to go too near the edge and have the wheels stuck. The moon, though only half, was bright. All they could hear was the lapping of the river and an occasional bird call. Soon the unmistakable hulk of Caleb Brown appeared walking with two other men. Isaac had brought with him a spout lantern and made a signal.

'Any news?' asked Uncle John.

'Joseph Martin's keepin' watch from the George,' Caleb said. 'He says Tom Pike's in town and there's a meetin' behind the poor house. There's a barrel cart ready, just the one.'

'We need to get closer and watch for 'em moving. Any hint as to where the goods are?' Uncle John continued.

'Only that they're close by,' David Preston said.

Uncle John laughed. 'Under everyone's noses no doubt.'

'An' Tarrant havin' the Dragoons huntin' to no avail,' David added.

The pony harnessed to John's trap snorted.

'Come on. We'll hide behind the Priory. We can watch from there,' Isaac said. 'Get the leathers on the nag's hooves, and on the wheels.'

One by one, they made their way beside the muddy Quomps towards the quayside and the old mill. They tied up the pony and trap, hoping it would look as though it belonged to the miller. Isaac, Caleb and Moses Pilgrim crept along the mill stream and hid themselves amongst some trees. Taking the lamp, David set out with Uncle John to watch for the other gang gathering behind the poor house. They hid amongst a clutch of cottages from where they could just make out what was going on. The smell of wood smoke from nearby chimneys filled the air. A baby was crying somewhere. Far enough from the poor house, so as not to be seen by the lamplight shining through the windows, stood a barrel cart, its canvas hood lit like a ghostly shroud in the moonlight. The mumbles of the men could barely be heard. Two men climbed onto the seat and with the lamps left unlit the cart started to move. Uncle John and David watched from the shadows as it set off towards them. The roll of the wheels in the gravel was muffled with leather - they'd used the same smuggler's trick to mask the sound. They saw the cart reach the top of the lane which met the road in front of the poor house. The cart turned right, towards the mill. Then to their surprise it turned into the Priory grounds. They dashed to the other side of their cottage hiding place. Uncle John turned the lamp towards the clump of trees where the others were hiding. He uncovered and covered the spout, twice. Seeing the signal, Isaac, Caleb and Moses crept towards them. They met in a hollow in the wall beside the old Lodge.

'They're in the graveyard!' Uncle John whispered. 'Quiet as we can. Let's find 'em first, then wait 'til they're busy on their task.'

The others nodded. Caleb was holding a club, Moses had a pistol. Slowly they edged along the shadowy wall. Then they moved swiftly into the darkness of the porch. From there they could just make out Ginn's gang at work in the flickering lamplight. The cart had been left close to the ancient building.

'Now!' growled Uncle John.

The five charged across the grass dodging the gravestones.

'Stand back or bear the price,' yelled Uncle John.

Caleb lifted his weapon in readiness and Moses pointed his pistol towards the group of men gathered around a grave. One of the men charged forward wielding a club. He hit out at Caleb. Caleb swung his club and caught the man hard on his arm. The man screamed out in pain but found the strength to strike at Caleb again.

'Stop, Guy!' Tom Pike's voice rang out into the darkness, echoing. 'Who be ye?'

'Hand over the goods, they belong to Sir Charles Tarrant,' shouted Uncle John, moving slowly towards Pike.

Isaac, Caleb, David and Moses inched after him.

'Take care, John,' Isaac whispered. 'They'll all be armed.'

'So, it ain't you, John Hewitt,' Pike said, lifting a fiery torch.

'What do ye mean?' Uncle John snarled.

'Ye've not got to these goods.'

The men by the graveside turned, the moon threw a moody light onto faces that were mean and scowling.

'The goods, none of us'll have 'em. They're gone. There's got to be another gang about.'

## Chapter 28

# Will's big decision

Will pulled on his oar until the *Solomon* caught the water flowing fast out of the Run. Guy Cox had had an accident last night, Master Hardyman had told him when he arrived at the Quay. So there was work at sea for him today. He'd rather do this than go back to Cliff House to do Scott's job. The day was bright and breezy, and the salt air was stinging the cut on his face. It had dried but he'd have a scar. But worse was the thought of it going bad and him dying, just like his father had. He'd wanted adventure and now he wasn't sure it was worth it. 'Why does Edmund Tarrant hate me so much?' he thought. 'For all his money he's stupid. Perinne is rich but she's clever.' Will smiled to himself. Fancy her getting away from the big house without being noticed. She'd also had the sense to bring the sacks. 'And Danny, a middlin' sort, he just treats me like anyone else. It doesn't matter to either of 'em that I'm poor,' thought Will. Should he meet them later? What was there to meet about? Isaac and Uncle John had taken the boxes from the boat just as he was setting out to the Quay. They'd said that Danny and Perinne had told Danny's father where they were. He didn't know why. The large box from the Priory was already on the trap when they'd arrived. He still had the one hidden behind his bed in his room though, so his friends hadn't mentioned that. But they'd all said that without this one the machine wouldn't work. He'd have to decide what to do about it.

Danny was sitting in the hallway of Cliff House again. Last time it was for fighting with Edmund, now it was for being out in Christchurch at night with Perinne. He hadn't seen Perinne since they'd been caught and it was his father who'd told him that Will hadn't returned to his new job in the stables.

The door to the library opened and Danny's father signalled to him. Inside was Sir Charles, sitting at his desk. Sir George was sitting in the chair next to a roaring fire. Then Perinne entered with her father, who was carrying one of the smaller boxes similar to the ones they'd found. Perinne stood next to Danny and gave him a smile.

'No sign of young Will Gibbs then, James?' Sir Charles asked.

'No, sir, but we think we know why he hasn't arrived.'

'Please tell me not Edmund again.'

'I'm afraid so, sir.'

As his father and Sir Charles were speaking Danny glanced around the room. He nudged Perinne and nodded towards the corner by the window. Yves was placing the box he'd been carrying with others that were stacked together in the corner of the room.

Sir Charles stood, turning his attention to the two children.

'I'm astounded,' he said. 'I've had my best men and dozens of Dragoons out looking for these and three children have done better.' He shook his head.

'I should be extremely angry. You were all in great danger. If the other gang had found you, well, only the

Lord above knows what would have happened to you. You know that I have put a price on the heads of Pike and Millar, to have them brought to the assizes. They'll both hang and the matter will be done with. But enough of that, I have to thank you and I will think of a suitable reward.'

'When will the boxes go to America?' Danny asked.

'At the soonest opportunity.'

'May I go with the boxes to the ship?'

'Oh, I would like that also,' Perinne said.

Sir Charles took a deep breath. 'After your good work, I'm sure that can be arranged.' He smiled at the pair and motioned his hand towards the door. 'You may go.'

He watched as they left the room and turned to see Yves looking at the boxes.

'It seems that all has worked out well, but we have a problem still,' said Yves.

'What is it?' asked Sir Charles.

'We have twelve boxes, but the principal box is missing.'

'The thirteenth box? Then where is it?' Sir Charles gasped.

There was silence.

Sir George spoke first. 'Well, Charles, I shall take the goods as they are, you'll still get your payment. There's a ship going out to Newfoundland the day after next. I'll arrange passage. This other box must be somewhere. Should it appear, send it to me in London and I'll have it sent on.'

'But box number thirteen has the most important components,' said Yves. 'It is probable that the machine cannot be made without the things it contains and then this whole venture will have been for nothing.'

Perinne and Danny made their way to Muddiford. Perinne had decided to leave Pierre behind. Danny couldn't ride and had refused to try.

'So, our adventure is over,' Perinne said.

'Yes. What will we do now? Could there be other mysteries to solve?' Danny replied.

'I should think that there will always be mysteries.'

'The mystery of why Edmund hates Will. Uncle John says it was lucky he was near Will's house last night.'

'It is strange. It is as though he is afraid, or even jealous. But also, I saw Uncle Charles hit him. This is where he learns it.'

'I've had punishment from my father, but it doesn't make me a bully.'

'Well, Edmund is to be sent away to school. Maman told me. We can tell this to Will and he can work at Cliff House after all.'

They reached the cliff top, then made their way down to the beach. There was no sign of Will. The sun started to set and the air was becoming chilly. A cold breeze blew around their faces.

'I'll walk back with you,' Danny said. 'I'll call in at the George after school tomorrow and see if Beth knows why Will didn't come. It would be good if he could come with us to the ship on Friday.'

When Will left the *Solomon* the following afternoon he was cold and wet. They'd gone out to fish despite the wind and the rain. Then Master Hardyman had told him Guy Cox would be returning the next day. 'There'll be nets to mend, Will, but not until Monday,' he'd said. When he arrived home the house was in darkness. Sam was outside and came towards him gingerly, his bruising still hurting him. He was surprised when he saw Beth inside. She was trying to light the fire but the tinder was damp.

'Yer friend Danny called in the George askin' after ye,' she said. 'He says they missed ye at the beach an' would ye be goin' again tomorrow. I told him ye were probably workin'!'

Will nodded. 'Where's mother?'

'Wi' Isaac.'

'Isaac?'

'Seems she thinks he's a kind of hero, comin' to your aid and then goin' off to Cliff House takin' them boxes.'

Will took the tinder box from his sister and managed to get a spark. He was starving. Until the fire got going, there'd be nothing hot for him. He drank some water and ate some bread and cheese. He made his way up the steps to the attic room and undressed. He climbed under his bedcovers to try to warm up. It wasn't quite dark and streaks of light leaked into the space. The damp creaked in the thatch. He pulled the woollen blanket around his shoulders. Was this how it would always be? Would the apprenticeship Sir Charles had offered only be stable work? And his mother - what was she thinking of with Isaac for goodness sake? He tossed and turned, his mind running over dreams of a better life. Before he finally fell asleep, he'd made a decision.

He woke early and stepped out of bed. He drew aside the drape. He could barely see but was used to rising in the dark, his eyes soon adjusting to the chinks of light. There was no sign of his mother but Beth was sound asleep. As quietly as he could he opened the drawer until it was completely out, then he reached for his tin of coins. He dressed, gathered his few clothes and placed them in a small trunk that had been his father's, then stretched across his bed and reached for the box hidden in the space behind. He put it into the trunk and crept down the steps.

He went into the back room. There was some meat on the table. Beth must have brought it back from the George. He took a slice and ate it, then stored the remainder away in the cupboard. He slipped into his boots and opened the back door. 'Sam,' he whispered. The dog came scampering into the cottage. Will stroked his long coat then gently ran both his hands down Sam's soft ears. 'You'll be fine, boy.' With tears prickling his eyes Will pulled on his coat, wrapped his scarf around his neck and pushed on his hat. He made his way through to the front and left, closing the door quietly behind him. It would take two or three hours to walk across Bourne Heath to Poole where, hopefully, there'd be a ship.

## Chapter 29

# A shock on the way to Poole

Will decided to walk along the cliff top. It was strange not having Sam around his heels but he'd be better off at home with Beth. How would he have fed him? He'd only a few pounds for himself. He felt the tin safe in his pocket. The sun was behind him but still low. He turned and looked out over Christchurch Bay. Ships, several with billowing sails like clouds, dotted the sea. This was his workplace, if he was lucky. Some of the ships would be heading east for Southampton, others west to Poole. Maybe the one he'd take was out there. He hoped to work a passage to America, as paying would take at least three pounds. If he could find a better job there, he could have money sent to his mother and Beth to come and join him. He drew the collar of his coat around his neck against the morning's chill and walked on along the track.

Danny was to wait by Staple Cross. He stood with his hands in his pockets and was blowing jets of breath, trying to make shapes. Crows cawed above, flapping around the crop of nests high in the trees. As he watched the lane he saw a cart approaching. As it neared he could make out Uncle John driving, his father sitting beside him. They swayed as the cart rolled along the rutted track, its wheels crunching in the mud and gravel. Behind it, tall and elegant, was Sir Charles's coach. Danny waved.

'You be goin' in the coach with Miss Perinne,' Uncle John said as he pulled up the two horses. Ben the stable boy jumped from the coach and opened the door, pulling down the step. Danny smiled as he noticed John Scott was coachman. Inside Perinne was sitting with her father. Sir George Cook was facing them. He patted the seat beside him and Danny climbed in and joined them. He grinned at Perinne.

'You haven't heard from your young friend then, Daniel?' Sir George asked.

The coach jolted as it set off.

'No, sir. His sister says he'll be working.'

'That's a shame. But you'll be able to tell him all about it.'

'The machine, Sir, do you think the man in America will be able to make it work?'

Sir George pressed his lips together into a line. 'I'm not sure. I do hope so. But we don't have all the parts.'

'Oh?' Danny said. 'Were there more?'

'Just the one, the thirteenth box, it wasn't with the others. Perinne's parents had a note written in the inventor's own hand that this was the most important of all the boxes.'

'Danny looked over to Perinne who shrugged her shoulders.'

'Haven't you told them, Perinne?'

'It is the first time that I have heard this,' she said.

'Do you know something, Perinne?' Yves asked.

'Well, yes, papa. Will has the box. I thought that he would have given it to Danny's Uncle.'

'I'm not sure Will was there when they collected the boxes you found. He did have that dreadful fight with

Edmund Tarrant too - maybe he forgot about the other box,' Sir George said.

'We can call at his house,' Danny suggested. 'We have to go through the town.'

'Good idea, young man. And if he's there he can come along after all.' Sir George rapped on the window and John Scott drew back a small glass panel. 'Shout for the cart, Scott.'

The coach halted and Uncle John's face appeared at the door.

'Take us to young Will's house please, Mr Hewitt. We think he has something we need.'

'Aye, sir,' Uncle John said, tipping the edge of his hat.

The coach came to a stop close to the end of a lane of lowly cottages. Uncle John appeared again.

'This is the place, sir.'

Sir George, Danny and Perinne climbed out of the coach and followed Uncle John nearly to the end of the track to an old and scruffy cottage. The thatch was green with clumps of moss. Shoots from weeds were poking through the earth around the doorway. There was an awful smell.

'Woof!'

'Sam!' Perinne shouted.

The dog bounded over to her, his tail wagging back and forth.

Sir George rapped on the door with his cane and Meg appeared.

'Mistress Gibbs,' Sir George began, 'I'm Sir George Cook. We're looking for Will.'

'What's happened? Is he in trouble?'

'No, but we think he can help us.'

Sir George smiled and stepped into the cottage. Danny and Perinne followed him. Danny couldn't believe the inside. The fireplace held a pool of ash and the room was cold and damp. A rug in front of the fireplace was threadbare. A stool and two chairs were set beside it and there was a small shabby table. If Danny was surprised Perinne was even more so. She'd never seen such a poor place. Even the Scott's cottage was better than this.

'We believe that Will found a box. It belongs with the others that he and his friends here found. It is the most important of all the boxes and I'll reward him well for its return.'

Meg smiled.

'I'm sorry, sir, but he 'aint here. But his sister be. I'll see if she knows 'bout this box.'

Beth had been listening at the top of the steps and came half way down. She smiled at Danny.

'I know about it sir. I'll fetch it for ye.' She disappeared again.

Danny could hear shuffling from above the ceiling, then a bang. After a few moments Beth appeared again. Her face was white and her dark eyes wide.

'Is everythin' all right our Beth?' Meg asked, walking over to the steps.

'The box ain't there, mother, and nor are Will's things. His clothes have gone, and father's trunk, too.'

Meg fell back onto one of the chairs. 'His clothes missing? Oh, Beth, where's he gone?'

Perinne stepped over to Meg and put her arm around her. She looked at Beth who had started to cry.

'I am sure that he will be all right, Madame,' Perinne said. 'Danny and I will look for him. We are good at solving mysteries.'

'Oh, Miss, wherever could he be?'

Sir George stepped forward. 'Will is a strong, brave young man. I'm sure he'll be fine. Have you had a falling out?'

'Why no, sir, but he were mighty upset over Edmund Tarrant attackin' 'im,' Meg sniffed.

'We need to get to Poole or we will miss the ship.' Sir George took a deep breath as he gathered his thoughts.

'We'll call again on our way back. If Will hasn't returned I'll see what I can do.'

'Thank you, sir. It's very kind.'

'Danny, Perinne, are you still coming?'

The pair looked at each other. Danny's stomach hurt - where was Will? But he didn't want to miss seeing the boxes onto the ship.'

'Yes, sir.' He turned to Meg. 'Mistress Gibbs, we will call back, I promise.' Then he turned and smiled at Beth.

The cart and coach rattled down the hill into Poole. The vast harbour spread out in front of them and ships' masts pointed to the sky like pine trees that had lost all their needles.

'Now, you two,' Sir George started. 'There'll be a lot of folk about and you'll need to keep close to me. Your fathers will be busy.'

They reached the dockside and Yves and James set out to find the *Majesty*. The harbour was buzzing with activity. Surly men trundled by, pushing hand carts, larger carts were pulled by horses. Others bustled back and forth carrying boxes, sacks and barrels. The sky was a chilly blue and gulls screeched in the salty air. Perinne and Danny walked behind Sir George, wondering at the height the masts reached. They soon caught up with their fathers who were talking to a tall man in high boots and long jacket, his tricorn hat edged with gilt braid.

'He's a pirate!' Danny whispered to Perinne.

Perinne giggled and put her hand to her mouth to stop herself from laughing.

Nearby a pale, bent man was standing with another man with a pox-marked face. They watched as Uncle John and

John Scott lifted the boxes off the cart and stacked them. The smaller ones had been tied together. Then suddenly a loud shout rang out across the track. An argument had broken out at a nearby alehouse. Danny and Perinne turned to look across and Perinne gasped.

'What's wrong?' Danny asked.

'Look, over there.' Perinne pointed to the side of the inn at a figure sitting on a small trunk. 'It's Will!'

Chapter 30

# The thirteenth box

Perinne dashed off. Danny tried to catch his father's attention, but he and Yves were deep in conversation with the ship's captain.

'Perinne!' Danny ran after her.

'Will!' Perinne shouted.

Will looked over his shoulder, his face a mixture of surprise and irritation. He turned his back to the quayside, bowed his head and stared at the ground.

'Will, you are here. How did you know?'

'Know what?'

'That we were bringing the boxes today.'

Danny had caught up with her. 'What's wrong?' he asked. 'Beth says all your clothes have gone.'

Will rubbed his hands together and blew into them.

'Ye've been to me 'ome?'

'Yes, we were looking for the thirteenth box, we thought you'd given it to Uncle John but it's missing.'

'Tis 'ere,' Will said, tapping the trunk. 'I thought if so many people were fightin' o'er it I could sell it – it'll pay for a passage if I can't work for it.'

'Passage? Where?'

'Newfoundland.'

Perinne and Danny glanced at each other and then back at Will.

'Why do you want to go there?' Perinne asked.

'What's 'ere? You've seen where I live. I've no work.' Will stood and turned to face his friends. Perinne gasped. The cut on Will's face was healing, but it ran from under his left eye around his cheek to his lips, there was also a nick on his chin.

'Why should I stay? I could be dead soon.'

'Is this about Edmund Tarrant?' Danny asked.

'I'm goin' to America, to make me fortune and show the gentry who can live in grand places.'

'What's wrong, Danny?' James Clarke had now arrived with Yves and Sir George.

'Will!' James said. He gazed astonished at the gash. 'Is that what Edmund Tarrant did to you?'

Will didn't answer.

'He's going to America, father!'Danny said.

Perinne grabbed her father's arm. 'Do not let him go papa. Can we help Will?'

'I'm not going 'ome.' Will turned to Sir George. 'Is the machine yer's?'

'Let's say I'm its guardian, young man,' Sir George said.

'Well, I've the box yer lookin' for.'

'Then I shall richly reward you for its return.'

Will smiled for the first time, then winced as the cut hurt.

'But your mother is fretting. Come back with us, we'll see to it Edmund keeps away.'

'That's what I were told before, but it didn't stop 'im.'

'He's being sent away to school,' Danny said. 'Come on, Will, come back with us. Perinne and I were talking about solving more mysteries.'

'Isn't one enough for ye?'

'Listen, Will.' Sir George put his hand on Will's shoulder. 'I've heard such a lot about you, finding Danny, rescuing Perinne. You should come home.'

221

'Goin' to Newfoundland would gi' me a chance to make somethin' o' me life,' Will said.

'Well, if you're determined to go then you can look after the machine. It sails on the *Majesty* for Newfoundland today. I'll arrange it with Captain Brice and I'll speak with Lady Elizabeth, ask her whether regular work can be found for your mother.' Sir Charles shook his head and let out a sigh. 'I'll make sure both she and Beth are all right, but how I shall tell them where you've gone, I'm not certain.'

The three men made their way back across the track to the ship, leaving the youngsters to say their goodbyes. Uncle John was standing chatting with John Scott and Ben was sitting on the cart.

'I'm sorry, Danny, Perinne. Ye're both good friends, but I'm not sure I want to come back. Please, go. I need to think.'

Perinne couldn't hold back her tears. She threw her arms around him and hugged him. Danny watched his friends. He felt like crying too. Maybe Will was right to go and try to make a better life for himself. In fact, he envied the notion of travelling to another country.

'Come on, Perinne.' Danny touched her arm softly. 'Let Will decide.'

'Adieu, Will.' She kissed his cheek.

Then Danny also put his arms around his friend. 'The coach is over there, Will. It's up to you. But if you do go, I expect you back within a year a rich man.' He smiled and Will smiled back.

Will watched his friends join Sir George and their fathers, and he thought about his own father. 'If I go, I'll let him down,' he thought. His mind went through the same worries that had churned in his head over the past few days. 'What will mother and Beth do? Surely Sir George would keep his word about watching after them. Can they manage alone? And why should the loathsome bully Edmund Tarrant win?' Also, he'd made that promise to his father. He stooped, opened the worn, brown trunk and took out the thirteenth box. 'What's so important about this?' he thought. He looked at the writing and remembered the golden cogs and copper coil he'd seen inside. The most important parts, Perinne had said.

Without warning, a skinny hand lunged, making a grab for the box. It was a man with a fearsome face, pox-marked and crimson with effort. His eyes were screwed into slits menacingly and his long hair was flying wildly under his round felt hat.

'Gi' that t' me!' the man snarled with reeking breath.

'Hey, get off me!' Will yelled. Will pulled the box towards him, grasping it tightly and tried to push the man away. 'Who is it?' he thought. He had a familiar look, but how would he know someone like this? People had stopped and had now gathered to watch what was going on.

'Come on, Will, gi' me the box.'

'Who be ye? 'ow d'ye know me name?' Will shouted.

'Ye father, we, er... worked together, years ago. C'm on give it to me and there'll be no bother, else I'll get thee back for that whack on the noddle thee gave me.' The man kept looking over his shoulder as though he expected help, but no one came.

Will glared at him. 'Who is he? I'd hit him on the head?' He tried to think.

Across the busy road Sir George Cook was climbing into the Tarrant coach. He turned to the noise. 'Look, James, Yves, someone's attacking young Will!'

'Hey! Leave him alone.' James Clarke cried out as he and Yves sped over towards the scene. Danny and Perinne jumped down from the coach and followed quickly.

'Leave him be!' James repeated.

Danny and Perinne had pushed their way through the onlookers and Danny gasped with horror. 'It's the kidnapper, father. That's the man who took Perinne!'

'Tom Pike!' Will screamed. 'That's how ye know me!

Why did ye take 'er? Were it fer this?' Will lifted the box high above his head.

'Seize him!' Yves bellowed. 'There is a price on his head!'

A woman screamed. Pike turned on his heels and, pushing away anyone in his path, he fled towards the quayside. James and Yves tried to give chase, but some people in the crowd started to panic, crashing into one another as they blindly tried to move out of the way. Just as James and Yves struggled through the tangle of people, a passing carriage drove directly across their path, causing them to leap back to avoid going under the wheels. They could see Pike in the distance looking round to check if he'd got away from them, grinning in triumph at his escape. But as he turned back towards the quay, Pike's jaw dropped in horror as he stared straight into the barrel of Captain Brice's pistol.

When James and Yves caught up with Pike he was already having his hands tied together. Then, cheered on by a group of sailors, they marched the smuggler away towards the gaol at King Street in hope of finding a constable.

'They've got him!' Danny shouted. 'Let's go and see where they take him.' Danny ran off.

'Come on Will,' Perinne urged. But Will shook his head. Seeing his reluctance, Perinne chased after Danny. But within minutes they were spotted by their fathers who sternly signalled to them to go to the coach, where Sir George was waiting. Danny, frustrated, beckoned at Will to join them.

Still clutching the box, Will picked up his trunk. As he approached the quayside he stopped and gazed over to the *Majesty*. Its two masts poked the clear blue sky. The white sails were furled and the cordage splayed like a spider web. There was a row of dark gun ports along the side and windows decorated the quarterdeck at its stern. The smell of the briny harbour filled his lungs. It would be sailing soon. It wasn't long before high tide. Will knew the rest of the boxes had been loaded, he'd watched Uncle John and the sailors take them aboard. He approached Sir George.

'Pardon, sir, may I speak wi' ye?' he asked, looking intently at the now bemused gentleman.

Danny and Perinne had already stepped into the coach expecting Will to follow them. Instead they turned to see their friend talking with Sir George, who was nodding as if he were agreeing with what Will was saying. They saw them set off towards the huge ship. Moving over to the opposite window of the coach to get a better view, the pair looked on as Captain Brice appeared and watched as hands were shaken.

Will was still holding the thirteenth box as he strode up the gangway. As he reached the top he stopped. Slowly he turned and gazed ashore, he seemed to be suspended, as if in a dream. Then he took a deep breath, turned and climbed aboard the ship.

# About *The Thirteenth Box*

## The mysterious machine

The telephone was invented in 1876 by Alexander Graham Bell. But other people were also trying to invent such a device. American inventor, Elisha Gray, also filed a patent and Italian man, Antonio Meucci, also invented a telephone in 1871, but didn't renew his patent.

Signals were first transmitted in France in the late 18th century and it is not impossible that the thoughts of inventors were turning to creating a machine to help people to talk to each other across distances. However the machine in *The Thirteenth Box* is simply an invention for this book.

## Smuggling and Christchurch

In the 18th and early 19th centuries Christchurch was an ideal place for smugglers. The town's geographical location on the coast with its beaches and large harbour with narrow entrance was ripe for bringing in contraband.

The large navy cutters (ships) were too big to get through the Run at Mudeford – spelled Muddiford on maps at the time. Here was the site of the famous Battle of Mudeford in 1784.

The harbour was large, plus Stanpit Marsh has inlets where the smugglers could hide. The most famous one is Mother Sillers Channel, which enabled goods to be landed at The Ship in Distress public house in Stanpit.

## Why did people smuggle goods?

England was at war. Across the Atlantic battles of the American War of Independence were taking place and many soldiers were there fighting. Taxes were being raised to pay for the war. There was no tax on what people earned (income tax) in 1780 and money was raised by paying duty (tax) on goods coming into the country. By smuggling the payment of duty was avoided. Smugglers were also called Free Traders because of this. Tea, brandy, silks and many other items were smuggled. Smuggling took place all around England's coast. The war also meant that there were few soldiers to guard the shores from smuggling. Customs Officers and Riding Officers were employed. The nearest customs houses to Christchurch were at Poole and Southampton. But the riding officers were usually local men who often turned a blind eye to the smuggling.

# Glossary

Life was quite different in 1780 when our tale is told. Here are some of the words, people and places you will find in this story.

*Anker* – A small barrel, usually containing brandy

*Bone Box* – An 18th-century term for the mouth

*Cod's head* – A rude insult, meaning a stupid person

*Contredanse* – A French version of English country dances, where couples danced in lines

*Dinner* – Dinner was the main meal of the day and was eaten in the late afternoon. Other meals were breakfast and supper.

*Dragoons* – Soldiers. The Dragoons in Christchurch didn't actually arrive until the 1790s, when the barracks were built. Any soldiers at the time would have lived with local families or in ale houses, but mostly they were abroad fighting.

*Fart followers* – a rude name for footmen whose job could include following behind their masters and mistresses, sometimes holding their coats to prevent them getting covered in mud and dirt.

*Free Grammar School* – the school Danny attended was held in St Michael's loft in Christchurch Priory. The boys would start very early and would often be chosen for their voices as they also sang at services. The loft is a now a small museum. Also, it is said signals were given from here to the smugglers out at sea – and you can still see the little window from where the signals were sent.

*Ice House* – These were pits dug into the earth often with a brick dome. Ice from rivers and ponds would have been placed in the pit and covered with straw to keep it as long as possible. Food was kept cold and ice used in ices.

*Leather coverings* – were used by smugglers on cart wheels and to cover horses' hooves, to make them as quiet as possible when moving smuggled goods.

*Middling* – People neither rich nor poor. More people at this time were becoming trades people and merchants with a reasonable income.

*Mr Brander* – Gustavus Brander was a fellow of the Royal Society and a Trustee of the British Museum. He built the house which is now Priory House. His archaeological excavations of the cliffs at Highcliffe and Barton resulted in the collection of fossil shells still stored at the Museum. He also excavated the ruins of the Priory buildings destroyed on the orders of Henry III.

*Mr Clingan's Trust* – This is a charity set up in Christchurch in 1746 by John Clingan to help the boys and girls of Christchurch into apprenticeships. It still exists today and young people can apply for small grants, particularly to help with studies.

*The Necessary* – Perinne's polite term for the toilet. Some grand houses had the first water closets at this time. Toilets were holes in the ground, sometimes covered with wooden boards with holes to sit on. People had chamber pots, kept under the bed, to use at night time. Poor people would have dung heaps close to their houses.

*Noddle* – Head

*Ostler* – This is a stableman who would look after the horses at inns

*Poor House* – Where people who could not support themselves would live. This could be whole families or orphans. In Christchurch, the Poor House became the Workhouse and is the building that is now the Red House Museum.

*Press Gangs* – Press gangs were used to recruit sailors for the navy, but many were violent. Gangs of men would offer a shilling – the King's shilling – but men were often tricked and taken against their will. The rules were men had to be between 18 and 55 years old.

*Reverend Jackson* – Reverend William Jackson was Vicar of Christchurch from 1778 to 1802. The character Adam Jackson is an invention for the story.

*Riding Officers* – men employed to try to prevent smuggling, though most were local men and involved in the trade.

*Small beer* – this was the name for a very weak beer and was given to children. Water was not very clean and small beer was often a safer drink.

*Smugglers* – People did not pay income tax in 1780 so to raise money for the country – mainly to pay for wars – duty was payable on items brought in from abroad. This made many items expensive and smugglers brought goods into the coves and harbours of the coast of Britain to sell and make money. Many people depended upon smuggling to live.

*Spout lamp* –These lamps were used by smugglers to signal to each other. They had a spout on the side which was covered and uncovered when the lamp was lit it.

*Tallow* – Tallow was made from animal fat and was used to make candles. Beeswax candles were more expensive and tallow was often all the poor could afford, but it smelled bad!

*Tea* – Yes, you all know what tea is – but did you know that in the 18th century it was very expensive? Tea was often kept in boxes with locks! Tea was one of the things most commonly smuggled.

*Venturers* – People, mostly wealthy, who funded smuggling by providing boats and other help.

# Places in Christchurch

Here are places in Christchurch mentioned in *The Thirteenth Box* that you can still visit (v) or see:

**Christchurch Priory** & **St Michael's Loft** (School room) (v)
**The Red House Museum** (Poor House) (v)
**Place Mill** (v)
**The Castle** (v)
**The Old House** (the Constable's House) (v)
**The George** (v) public house
**The Eight Bells** (v) shop
**The Ship** (v) public house
**The Ship in Distress** (v) public house
**The Marshes** (Stanpit Marsh) (v)
**Mudeford** (v)
**Quomps** (v)
**Dr Quartley's house** still stands but is a private residence.


There remain some old cottages in Burton similar to the one Danny would have lived in.

Will's old cottage would have stood near to the by-pass where a car park now stands.

There was no such place as Cliff House. There was a building called High Cliff and this was replaced in the early 19th century by Highcliffe Castle.

The Bargate was destroyed in 1744 but there is a road, Bargates, in the town centre.

The Thirteenth Box is the first book in the
A SMUGGLERS' TOWN MYSTERY series

Coming next ...

# The Face of Sam

## Chapter 1

# Shipwreck

'The coat, get the coat!'

The little girl turned her face towards the sound of a gruff voice. The sky was black. The rain had stopped but the wind still lashed and waves were crashing like thunder onto the shore around her. She could feel the water rolling over her legs and back again. Sand stuck to her cheeks and her lips were dry and salty. Shouts bellowed amongst the sound of the sea as a large shadowy figure loomed towards her. She lay, motionless, opening her mouth to shout 'help', though nothing came out.

'C'mon!'

The girl watched, helpless as the huge figure bent towards her and began to unbutton the sodden, woollen garment. She had no strength to fight the man off.

'But tis only a girl,' he shouted back over his shoulder.

'Get the coat.'

'Be still as ye can girl, fer ye life, don't speak a word.' the stranger whispered, as he scooped her up from the sands and threw her over his broad shoulder. She stayed limp, her arms dangling down the man's back like she were a deer he'd poached. His wet leather jacket smelled like fire and animal. The beach seemed full of the shadows of people and ponies and noise. 'Where's Mother?' she wanted to ask.

The man carried her across the sands and lifted her onto a waiting cart; her legs, cold, wet and unsteady could barely hold her. The moon peeked from behind a break in the cloud lighting up the man's bearded face. He lifted his finger to his lips then he pushed some small barrels to one side.

'Lay thee down girl, quickly now.'

She curled herself down beside the barrels, terrified but helpless as he covered her with some sacks. She could still hear shouting and felt the cart jolt as if other items were thrown in. Then the cart set off. The wheels struggled in the sand until finally they crunched onto gravel.

# Bibliography

## Local

Beamish, Dockerill, Hillier – *The Pride of Poole* 1688-1851 – Borough of Poole / Poole Historical Trust - 1974

Hoodless W A – *Old Town Halls of Christchurch* – Natula Publications 2009

Large J – *Stories of the New Forest* – John Large 1999

Powell M - *1784 The Battle of Mudeford* – Natula Publications 1993

Stannard M – *The Makers of Christchurch, A Thousand Year Story* – Natula Publications 1999

White A – *Christchurch Through The Years, Bargates, Fairmile and Barrack Road* – Allen White 1986

White A – *Christchurch Through The Years, Bridge Street & Purewell* – Allen White, Revised by The Red House Museum 2003

White A – *Christchurch Through The Years, Church Street and Castle Street* – Allen White 1985

White A – *The History of Christchurch High Street* – Allen White Revised by The Red House Museum

## General

Cockayn E – Hubbub, *Filth, Noise and Stench in England* – Yale University Press 2007

Grose F – *A Classical Dictionary of the Vulgar Tongue* – S Hooper 1785 (via Google Book Search)

Picard L - *Dr Johnson's London* – Weidenfeld & Nicholson 2000

Platt R – *Smuggling in the British Isles* – Tempus - 2007
Quennel M & CHB – *A History of Everyday Things in England Vol III* _ B.T. Batsford Ltd 1961
Styles J – *The Dress of the People* – Yale University Press 2007

## Other sources

Christchurch Local History Society, Local History Room
The Red House Museum and Gardens

## Paintings

A lot of information about the way people lived and of their clothes and belongings can be found in pictures painted at the time. Here are some of the artists whose pictures I looked at:

**George Morland**
**Thomas Gainsborough**
**Elizabeth Louise Vigée Le Brun**
**William Hogarth**

## The internet

www.britishmuseum.org
www.3.hants.gov.uk/archives
http://www.heritage.nf.ca/exploration/18fishery.html
http://www.smuggling.co.uk/
http://www.british-history.ac.uk/report.aspx?compid=42054

# The Author

## Julie Ratcliffe

Married with three adult sons, Julie is an honours graduate of the Open University (1988). She studied British social history and literature from 16th to 19th centuries, including comparative work between Britain and Europe and Britain and America. Julie is a full member of the Society of Women Writers and Journalists.

Julie has enjoyed writing from childhood. She began writing children's stories when working for Bolton Public Libraries, and often read her work to visiting school children. However, she never attempted to have the stories published. She continued to invent stories for her three boys, but it is only now that she has decided to publish her work.

Although born and raised in the north west of England, Julie has lived in Christchurch, Dorset since 1980. Here she has become fascinated with the history of this ancient town with its medieval relics, beautiful, cathedral-sized Priory Church, two rivers and quays. The town's development has been well-documented throughout the ages; Christchurch can trace its Mayors back to the 12th century.

Julie is a member of the Christchurch Local History Society and attends meetings of the Village Writers, who gather monthly in the New Forest.

**www.julieratcliffe.co.uk**

# Domini Deane

Domini Deane is a self-taught artist who has been designing magical worlds and creatures since she could pick up a crayon. After spending her childhood years in the Rocky Mountains of North America, she moved to Dorset, England, in 1998.

Most of Domini's illustrations are in watercolour, but she also enjoyed working in acrylics while designing her oceanarium-themed lion sculpture in the Pride of Bournemouth exhibit in 2011. Her art is noted for vibrant use of colours and exquisite detail.

Domini's work has been featured on several book covers and in various publications, including ImagineFX magazine. She is currently designing a Chinese zodiac collection and a series of multicultural angels. She has been illustrating several children's books for her mother (not yet published) and also plans to write her own someday.

For more information, please visit:

**www.dominideane.com**

# What readers say

*"I really enjoyed this book. It was really exciting and the best book I have ever read. My favourite character is Perinne. I think the author is a really good writer. I like the way it is based in a real place."*

Nicola, age 9

*"I really liked your book, The Thirteenth Box. My favourite character was Perinne."*

Isabel, age 10

*"I found her reading your book very late at night when she should have been asleep!"*

Rob, Isabel's Dad

*"As for the book, "The Thirteenth Box", although it's aimed at youngsters and I am not far off 81  it is one of the most enjoyable "unputtable down" quality books I have ever read.*

*The author has the talented secret in her writing which is that her characters come alive from the pages. One can see and hear in imagination the sounds and detect the smells even! Well I can anyway!"*

Lee

# The Thirteenth Box

National Self-published Book of the Year Award –
Runner up

Organised by *Writing Magazine* and the David St John
Thomas Charitable Trust

*'Magnificently produced' 'Fantastic attention to details.'*

**What the press say ...**

*'A cracking good adventure story ... nothing interferes
with a story led plot perfect for around 10-12s...'*

The School Librarian

*'The pace never lulls in this intriguing adventure that
throws light on times past.'* ★ ★ ★ ★

Bournemouth Daily Echo

*'...an exciting children's story of smuggling ... the well
thought out plot moves along quickly ...'*

Town and Village Times